Armored Hearts

Melissa Turner Lee

&

Pauline Creeden

An imprint of Topline Tack
Yorktown, Virginia

ISBN: 0615799302
ISBN-13: 978-0615799308

Dedication

For everyone who likes a little Fantasy with their History. And all those who have always loved Steampunk, but didn't ever know what it was….

Acknowledgements

We thank God for bringing us together – because as a team, we are stronger than either of us alone. But even a two-stranded cord is breakable without more support. So we'd like to give a shout out to our awesome editor, Sheila Hollinghead, to our many beta readers and people we bounced ideas off of. Thanks for helping make Gareth more likeable. and Jessamine awesome.

Chapter One

Twelve-year-old Tristan Gareth Smyth gripped the armrests of his wheelchair and said, "This will do. I can make it the rest of the way on my own from here."

His eyes trained up the landmark tree, and he had that stirring in his heart again. The vapor of a memory, maybe a dream. He always had that feeling when he looked up at the broad branches of this particular oak. Then he remembered who he was talking to and his face hardened.

The maid, Sarah, with her strong Scottish burr, patted him on the shoulder. Gareth refused to look at her. He stared down at his knee pants instead.

"Are ye sure ye will be all right? I dona mind walking with ye the rest of the way to Mr. Strong's house."

Gareth clenched his hands into fists. "I'll be fine."

"Too bad he didn't like coming out to the manor. Remember how green Mr. Strong got when he choked on me spice cake that day and ran off." She laughed but tried to cover it with a cough. "I thought that would be the end of 'im but he worked it out with yer grandfather to instruct ye in town. Funny, me spice didna bother the rest of ye."

She bent down in front of Gareth, attempting to make eye contact. "There are lots of children in this section of town. Her arms swept toward the houses along the road. "Ye might try making friends with 'em."

He turned away and clenched his jaw. Children never wanted to make friends with him. The chair made them uncomfortable. And what did he care anyway? He attempted to give her as stern a look as his grandfather would. "I know the way from here, and I won't be late. You can go on to market now."

The breeze picked up and blew wisps of red hair into the woman's round face. She smiled. "Oh, it's such a pretty day. This fresh air will do ye good, fer certain."

Was she making fun of him? Gareth scowled.

She patted her hands on her knees and stood straight again. "Well, then, I'll leave ye to it. I've got to run off to the baker's. Be sure to get to Mr. Strong's in a timely manner. Though I think yer old governess was doing a fine job. Not sure why ye need Mr. Strong. But I guess it's none of me concern."

She was a servant, in uniform, and he was the future Earl of Pensees. Following his instruction was her duty. She and her husband, Thompton, had been employed by his grandfather as far back as Gareth could remember, but regardless, they might find themselves out of work and heading back to Scotland if she kept voicing that sort of opinion.

No, Gareth could never really get them fired. But he'd make her think he could. He shook his head in the same disapproving manner he'd seen his grandfather use.

The sunlight played in the golden highlights of the woman's ruby hair. Although her green eyes twinkled, she continued to voice her cutting opinion. She placed one hand on his shoulder. "It's not being stuck in this chair that keeps ye lonely. It's yer surly attitude."

Gareth couldn't help but let his forehead scrunch a little. He crossed his arms and turned his face from her.

Her accent was thick and melodic, familiar in a way. His mother had been Scottish though he hardly remembered her. Still, Gareth kept his pout in place. The truth was, he didn't know how to relate to others. Even people who could feel at ease talking to perfect strangers stammered or spoke quickly to him and walked away. The wheelchair did more than keep him from playing.

She straightened the collar of his waistcoat. "Look, there's a little girl comin' now. She looks to be about Tabitha's age. Maybe a wee bit older."

He did glance then, but just under his lashes, not to give the impression that he cared. Easier to act like he didn't care than to show he truly did. He refused to give anyone more reason to feel sorry for him. No one pities an angry person.

He missed Tabitha...Tabitha Fitzgerald, his grandfather, Lord Gerald Smyth, Earl of Pensees's bastard daughter. But ward was her polite title. At five years old, she had been the only person he allowed to get close. Maybe it was the way she would climb up in his lap, never caring about the wheelchair. She didn't see it when she looked at him; she only saw Gareth.

He never spoke to Tabitha about who her parents really were, but she knew. For some reason, servants believed children to be both deaf and dumb and gossiped openly around them. That's how Gareth knew the truth about his own mother. He was told she died, but he'd overheard the maids say she had run back home to Scotland and how they didn't blame her. It's also how he'd learned the truth of his own father's death—shot by his mistress's jealous husband.

"I'm heading off. I'll be sure to get ye a sweet roll for later."

Gareth only grunted in response.

When the maid turned away, Gareth allowed himself to watch the little girl play. Her hair was a darker blonde than

Tabitha's and had streaks of amber. She looked to be a bit taller, too, as she ran around in a green day dress and stockings. She pushed a hoop along until she reached the tree. Once there, she looked both ways. Her eyes met Gareth's, and for a moment, he was tempted to turn away to keep her from doing it first. Instead, she smiled broadly and beckoned him closer.

Gareth wheeled his chair to the tree trunk, his curiosity getting the better of him. The girl dropped the hoop on the ground and took hold of the lowest branch. She whispered in an accent he didn't recognize, "Keep watch for me and call out if you see anyone coming."

His chin tucked in and his eyes grew wide. She took it as assent and nodded, starting her climb. She was spirited like Tabitha. The thought of being able to climb a tree at all pricked at Gareth's heart. He would never get to climb a tree.

Again he put on his bored expression. No one needed to know he was jealous of the girl. Gareth made a habit of never owning his true feelings. It was his protective covering. With his lids half closed, he tried not to watch the girl or keep an eye out for anyone else's approach. Without his permission, his gaze returned to the girl's powder-white limbs as she climbed higher than most children did.

Soon she was too high up.

Gareth adjusted himself in his seat, his eyes darting around. Instead of keeping lookout, he hoped for some adult to show up and tell the girl to come down.

The girl called in a harsh whisper. "Look! Watch this."

She scooted out on a branch, making her way to a bird's nest. The limb wobbled as she got closer to the end.

He was about to call out a warning to her when it was too late. The branch snapped. The little girl was falling with barely a squeal.

All Gareth could think was that he needed to do something. He rushed toward her and blinked. How? He didn't know how he had caught her but he had. Her giant, brown eyes grew as he held her, several feet above the ground. Then she looked down, and her eyes became wider. He swallowed hard and, in a rush, touched the ground, placed the girl on the grass, and flew back to his chair.

His heart still pounded in his ears as he sat. He tried to mask his confusion as he masked all other uncomfortable emotions, but it wasn't working. The girl stared at him, but said nothing as a dark-haired woman rushed toward her.

"Sweeting, are you ok?" The woman swept the girl up into her arms. "I got here as fast as I could. I can't believe you did that. I thought I told you not to climb that tree."

She put the girl back down and looked her over, grabbing her head and looking for a sign of injury. "Aren't you hurt at all? I saw you falling from the window upstairs."

The girl shook her head too quickly, like she was still in shock.

"Come on back to the house." the pinch-faced woman snapped, ushering the little girl away.

The girl yanked her hand free of the woman's grasp and rushed back to Gareth. She placed an object in his hand and kissed his cheek.

"You were amazing," she whispered and turned back to the woman who called out her name.

Gareth's cheeks burned. What did the woman say the girl's name was? He didn't hear with the blood rushing to his ear drums. Jessie? Jenny?

The woman scolded the girl as she returned to her. "What did you do? Where are your manners? You don't talk to cripples. Best to act like you don't see them at all."

The words struck Gareth like a bucket of cold water, but he let it slide off him as he thought about the fact that he had actually flown. He watched after the girl as her dark eyes stared back. His mind was muddled at what had happened. The muscles in his face hardened, and he stared at the woman's back as they retreated.

Shaking his head, he remembered he was supposed to be heading to Mr. Strong's house. He pushed the wheels of his chair down the road again. He'd forgotten he was holding something and nearly dropped it. The small, pale blue-green stone had a few dark wrinkles, but almost looked like a robin's egg. He put it to his nose. The flowery scent of the stone smelled just like the girl.

Gareth was so caught up in staring at how tiny the stone was in his palm, he'd forgotten all about Mr. Strong until the man called his name. "Master Tristan, what are you doing out here? You were to report to my house a quarter of an hour ago."

"I prefer Gareth." He narrowed his eyes at the pale, feeble man.

Mr. Strong ran a hand through his sparse, blond hair and smiled, his lips forming a thin line. "Yes, of course."

Mr. Strong placed himself behind Gareth's chair and pushed down the lane. "I have an excellent plan for your studies today. I see you've brought no supplies from your home but no matter. I have plenty of paper and pens to practice your lettering…"

Gareth rolled his eyes, knowing Mr. Strong couldn't see. The man's cheerful babble continued as he pushed him toward the house past the inn. The stone rolled between Gareth's fingers, and he remembered the feeling of the girl's lips on his cheek.

***

Gareth sat alone at dinner that evening, only picking at his plate. The long hardwood table seemed bigger than usual and the house was hollow and quiet with Tabitha away. Grandfather and Tabitha would be in London until the end of the month.

Grandfather could stay in town forever as far as Gareth was concerned. It was Tabitha he missed. His grandfather couldn't even look him in the eye. Every time Grandfather's hard gaze laid on Gareth, it accused him of falling short of what a legitimate heir should be. Accused him of being worthless because he was a cripple.

He swallowed hard and choked down the cold bite of food he'd taken. It clawed its way down his constricted throat. If only he could walk and run like the other boys. Then maybe he'd be at boarding school with them instead of the empty house. Or at least in London with Tabitha. He blinked hard when he remembered. *He could fly.*

But had he really flown? Maybe it was some sort of fantasy he'd let get out of control. But there was the little girl. She was too real to be fantasy. Her body had been warm and soft against his, and her giant, brown eyes had locked on him when he caught her. She'd smelled like flowers. He pulled the stone from his pocket and sniffed it again, closing his eyes.

It had to be real. If he flew once, could he do it again?

Gareth normally waited at the table for a servant to push him to the stairs, pick him up from his chair, and carry him to his chamber. He decided to wheel himself. The winding staircase of Waverly Park unfolded before him like an uncurled tongue. He glanced about, just as the little girl had done before climbing the tree.

First he thought the word 'fly,' but nothing happened. He tried lifting his rear off the seat and pushing himself forward, but let out a stifled yelp of pain as his shoulder hit the railing before he fell onto the red carpet on the stairs.

Gareth pulled himself by the railing and stood. His legs wobbled but held. He rubbed his upper arm. It was sure to sport a bruise the next day. Strange how he was able to kick and stand but not able to walk. He used his leg to pull the chair closer. No doctor could explain it. His grandfather accused him of faking—like Gareth would choose to be stuck in the blasted chair.

He narrowed his eyes at the ugly, brown, wooden chair on wheels that kept him separated from life. His grandfather took Tabitha to the city every few months. Gareth had never been. His grandfather said making accommodations for him and his chair was too much trouble. He was almost a grown man, and yet a male servant bathed him. He hated the chair.

Gareth glanced up the stairs toward his chamber door. He thought about how he wanted to be there—to go there on his own, without a servant carrying him and going back for his chair. He stared at the door and willed himself there.

The door drew closer and closer. He glanced down. The stairs lay beneath him along with his chair. He was floating upward and toward his bed chamber. He thought he heard a servant coming and willed himself to go faster, like he'd done that morning in order to catch the little girl.

He pushed the door open and flew inside, kicking the door behind him. It slammed shut. The freedom of this new discovery made his soul take flight. Gareth flew to the ceiling and got a close-up view of the cherubs there and smiled. That was a rare thing, for Gareth to smile with Tabitha away. Until that moment, she was the only one capable of pulling one out of him.

A knock came from the door. Gareth hurried his descent and was seated on the bed by the time the door opened. Sarah peeked in. "Lord Gareth, are ye in here?"

Gareth gave her his usual grumpy look. "Where else would I be?"

"But yer chair is still downstairs, and ye didna ring the bell fer Roberts. How'd ye get up here?"

Gareth's words stumbled on his tongue as he made up an answer. "I…he… walked by me at the bottom of the stairs, and I had him carry me up."

"He must'a fergot to go back fer yer chair. I'll go fetch it fer ye."

"No! I don't want it in here."

Sarah stepped in, her eyebrows furrowed. "Allow me to get ye ready fer bed."

"No! I'm old enough to do that myself, too."

"How?"

Gareth exploded. "I am the lord here when my grandfather is absent. Do not question me!"

Sarah bowed, eyes to the floor. "Yes, m'lord. Sorry fer bein impertinent." She left without looking up again and closed the door behind her.

Gareth bounded from his bed and grabbed hold of the wing chair in his room. He pushed it against his chamber door. His grandfather didn't allow him a proper lock. He circled around, hovering just above the floorboards. What to do next? His gaze fell on the balcony doors.

He flew toward them and threw them open. The breeze blew through the leaves of the tree across from the window. With a smile, he soared over the railing. Gareth had never been in a tree before. He'd envied the little girl that morning and her ability to explore. Now he had his chance.

But not this tree. It was small and weak. He wanted to sit in his favorite tree. It was dark so no one would be out and about in the town's square. He flew faster and faster through the graying darkness. The wind rushing through his hair tickled, and he laughed freely. Gareth blinked against the chill night wind.

Within minutes, Gareth found the town's square and settled on a tree limb. His favorite oak tree now had a new memory. The tree the girl had climbed that very morning. The tree he'd watched countless little boys climb. Now he was there.

He looked down the path toward the house the little girl had gone back into earlier. He'd have to find out who she was and convince her to keep his secret.

Gareth took off toward the house and peered into one of the upstairs windows, but the room was empty. The bed was made, and stark white sheets covered the rest of the furniture. He made his way to the next window. It, too, was dark and empty with dust sheets covering all the furniture. The whole house was devoid of life.

Was she a ghost after all? A phantom?

He fingered the stone in his waistcoat pocket. It was still there. Gareth heard a rustling sound below and looked down. Fear gripped at his chest at the thought of being discovered, but it was only a dog. It looked like Tabitha's speckled brown mutt.

Gareth left the town and soared over open pastures and empty fields. It wasn't until bats flew by and spooked him that he decided to go home.

He flew through his balcony doors. Standing in the middle of his room was wide-eyed Tabitha. Her orange tabby cat circled her legs.

"Gareth?"

His eyes shot to the door. The chair legs had made two deep scratches in the hardwood floor, and the door stood open only six inches. Enough for Tabitha to squeeze through. He quickly made his way to the door and slammed it shut. The chair nearly struck the floor. He righted it before flying to Tabitha and setting his feet on the floor in front of her. Blonde ringlets framed her face and fell into her eyes. Gareth pushed them aside, revealing round baby-cheeks.

"Hey, my favorite girl. Did you have fun in London?"

Her pupils nearly swallowed the blue of her eyes. She whispered, "You were flying. Like in the fairy stories Sarah tells me."

Gareth calmed his racing heart. Would treating flying as normal be the best way to deal with this? "Yes, it's a new trick I learned today. Want me to take you for a fly? It's even better than a ride in my chair."

She nodded enthusiastically and raised her arms to him. A smile grew on her lips. He lifted his little aunt to his hip and cradled her. "All right. But just a short trip around the room."

He held her close as he buzzed around the ceiling a half dozen times. He reversed his path to keep them both from growing dizzy.

She giggled wildly until he shushed her. "Now this must be our secret. You can't tell Lord Gerald or Sarah or anyone."

"Why not?"

Gareth lowered his feet to the ground and set Tabitha on the floor before sitting on the bed. He raised his brows causing his forehead to wrinkle for emphasis. "Because then it wouldn't be our secret. I never tell Lord Gerald about the animals you find and bring home, now do I?"

She shook her head. "No, you never do."

"So, can you keep this secret for me?"

Tabitha's cat pawed and scratched at Gareth's door. He flew over to it and quickly let it out. He turned back to face the blue-eyed, little girl looking up at him. "Can you promise?"

Her eyes were like giant blueberries. "Yes, I promise."

He patted her on the head. "Good girl. Now, why are you back already?"

"I told Lord Gerald I missed you too much."

The words pulled that string in his heart again, making him feel sad and happy at the same time. Gareth took her in his arms and held the child to his chest. "I'm glad you're back. I missed you, too. The house is empty with you gone."

A knock sounded at the door.

"Yes?" Gareth called out.

Sarah peeked in. "Have ye seen... oh there ye are, little missy. Come now. Time to get ready for bed."

Sarah stared at the grooves in the floor and eyed the chair sitting in an odd place. Her green eyes met his with a questioning glance, and he returned her look steadily. Neither said a word.

Tabitha took the maid's offered hand. Sarah dropped her eyes and lead the child out, closing the door behind her.

For the very first time in his life, Gareth dressed himself. After pulling the stone from the pocket, he wadded his waistcoat into a bundle and threw it in a corner. He set the stone in a special place on top of his wardrobe where no one would find it. With a nod, he settled himself on his bed, lying down and pulling up the covers.

A new sense of life filled Gareth. He'd need to be careful. The staff was more alert with the old man home.

Gareth smiled as he drifted off to sleep. He dreamed of flying off and never coming back. But another dream intermingled with that one, filled with a honey-blonde girl and large brown eyes.

A girl he'd never seen before and wondered if he'd ever see again.

Chapter Two

4 Years Later

Gareth watched nine-year-old Tabitha tuck bits of her dinner into her pockets as Grandfather spoke. *Treats for the mutt.* Gareth sighed and kicked her under the table. If Grandfather caught her, he'd ask her why, and then the dog would be discovered.

Tabitha's sky-blue eyes met Gareth's. They were just like his grandfather's eyes, but full of warmth and kindness. Gareth was the image of his father, except for the hazel eyes that belonged to his mother, or so he'd been told.

Gareth narrowed those eyes at his aunt, his look stern. She could sneak into the kitchen later and get something for the animals. He would help her keep her secret just as she'd kept his.

The old man was growing stingier by the day. He had rid Waverly Park of most of its fulltime staff just the month before. Thankfully, he'd kept Sarah for Tabitha's sake. She was fond of the maid and her husband. If Grandfather disposed of the dog and cat, Tabitha would be heartbroken, and Gareth couldn't allow that.

"And how are things in the parish?" Grandfather sliced the meat on his plate as he questioned the minister who came by every Tuesday to join them for dinner.

Reverend Piper sat up in his chair. "We've had several parishioners' homes robbed in the last week. Mrs. Duncan's silver spoons were taken along with Mr. Duncan's gold watch. It's dreadful. Just dreadful. These aren't people with pockets full of silver and gold to spare. Those items were keepsakes—heirlooms. Things they'd probably do better selling for a bite to eat—only to be taken by some hoodlums." He shook his head and bowed it.

"What's been done?" Grandfather asked in a bored tone and never glanced up from his dinner. He didn't really care about the locals.

"The authorities have been notified and are looking into it," Reverend Piper answered, with his mouth full. He swallowed hard and continued. "All the intrusions have been on the east side of the village. Most of those hit are farmers already struggling to make it. Something like this only brings spirits down further."

Tabitha chimed in, "What can be done for them?"

Her eyes were wide with concern. Gareth felt it too, but he kept it masked. He was more practiced at hiding his true feelings.

Grandfather glared at Tabitha, his expression stern. "Children are to be seen and not heard. If you cannot remember that, you will go back to dining in the nursery."

Tabitha's head bowed. "Yes, Lord Pensees."

Reverend Piper stammered, "It's sweet of the child to be concerned, don't you think?" He looked across the table at Tabitha. "We can pray that God will send help. A guardian to watch over the shire. And for someone to bring work to the town. Farming isn't sufficient for the people here any longer."

Tabitha peeked up at the minister but kept her head bowed. "I will pray for that now." She closed her eyes in silent prayer.

Gareth watched, amazed at her sweetness and faith. How could she keep it when she lived in a house run by Grandfather? Hard to believe she was related to the old man at all, the way she cared about stray animals and desperate people. All she could do was pray, and he knew she would do so every night.

Her sweetness and desire to help was contagious, and Gareth began to think and tune out the old men as they spoke.

***

Reverend Piper had left, and Grandfather had retired for the evening, but Tabitha was nowhere to be found. She normally waited by the stairs to keep lookout for Gareth so he could get himself to his room. He checked in Grandfather's office. He often found her there, practicing her arithmetic on parchment or glancing at some of the latest marvels pictured in the newspaper.

Gareth wheeled himself out of the empty study and around to look in another room, but she wasn't there either. He pushed the wheels through the open space of the foyer and into the hall toward the kitchen.

It wasn't proper for him to enter; it was below his station. But he pushed harder toward the room, regardless, once he heard Tabitha's weeping.

He watched from the open door of the kitchen. Sarah sat in a chair, cradling Tabitha in her lap. Sarah's orange curls were coming loose from her bun. "There's na ye can do fer the folk but pray. God will hear yer prayers, just as Reverend Piper said."

Tabitha sat back on the woman's lap and wiped her wet eyes. "How do you know?"

Sarah pushed blonde hair that had fallen into Tabitha's face behind the little girl's ear. "Because the Good Book says the prayers of the righteous avails much, and ye, me sweet girl, 'ave a good and righteous heart."

Boot steps moved toward the two of them from the other side of the kitchen. Gareth had not realized Thompton was there, too, until the tall lanky man with brown hair knelt in front of Tabitha and took her small hand in his. "It also says the angels assigned to wee lads and lasses go before the throne of the Almighty daily. So ye say yer peace to God and He will get the message. And ye can sleep well knowin' God heard ye."

Thompton grabbed Tabitha under the arms, picked her up, and swung her in a circle about the room, causing her to giggle with delight before he set her on the floor and knelt again before her. "And ye need be headin' to bed and sleep soundly, because not only do God's angels be watchin' over ye, but also the good fairies."

Tabitha grabbed the man around the neck and gave him a quick kiss on the cheek before giving one to Sarah.

"I'll be up to tuck ye in after I finish in here," Sarah said as she made her way to a stack of dishes.

Tabitha nearly ran into Gareth when she darted into the hall. Her eyes widened. "I'm sorry! I forgot to come watch for you."

Gareth smiled at his little aunt. "That's all right. I wasn't quite ready to go up yet anyway." He wheeled around and headed back in the direction he'd come from with Tabitha beside him.

"Why are you so worried about the townspeople?" Gareth asked as they headed for the stairs.

Tabitha shrugged, "I don't know. I guess I think about how awful it must be to have just enough to get by and have someone come and take it from you. It's just wrong." She ran around the stairs, then up them and back. She smiled and said in a loud whisper, "All's clear."

Gareth smiled back and took flight from his chair to his chamber door. The orange tabby appeared beside him and raced him up the stairs. Tabitha soon joined him in his chamber, the orange tabby cradled in her arms. She set it down, plopped herself in the wing chair, and picked up his math book. He was supposed to finish working some numbers for Mr. Strong before his time of instruction the next day.

"Can I finish these for you?" She glanced up under long, dark lashes.

"That would be cheating. Besides those are too hard for you, and arithmetic isn't healthy for the female mind."

"That's stupid and not true. I like numbers. Miss Duncan is teaching me higher arithmetic. She says I might need it someday if I end up a governess like her."

Gareth dismissed the notion with a shake of his head. "You'll find some gentleman to marry you and make you a lady. You won't need to think at all then."

Her face scrunched. "Maybe I don't want that. I like to think about more than pretty dresses and my hair. I'd rather spend my days teaching children than worrying about what color dress I should wear."

Honestly, neither could he imagine a girl who chewed her fingernails and hated having her hair braided would care about the color of her dress.

The cat pounced from the floor back into her lap, and she patted it absentmindedly. She let out a sigh. "I wish there was some way I could help the people in town."

Gareth furrowed his brow and floated a few feet above his bed. He liked the feeling of weightlessness that came from not touching the ground or his furniture.

Tabitha bowed her head in what looked like a silent prayer before opening her eyes and starting on Gareth's arithmetic anyway. "The way our finances are going, I will probably need to look for employment by my sixteenth birthday."

"Have you been looking in Grandfather's books again?"

"I can't help it. Working numbers is soothing." Tabitha pouted. "We are barely hanging on. I can't, for the life of me, figure out why Sarah and Thompton stay. Did you know Lord Gerald had to cut their pay by half, and they stayed anyway?"

Gareth blinked hard and lowered himself back to the bed. He had not known that. No wonder the other staff had left. He did know Grandfather had let out his home in London this year rather than visit for the season. They had little more than a title, and the farmlands barley produced. Times were changing, just like the turn of the century. Those in trade had more in their bank accounts than their landlords. If Tabitha were legitimate, she would be Lady Smyth, daughter of an Earl. That could help her secure a good union when she became of marrying age. But instead she was penniless Miss Fitzgerald of dubious origins.

Gareth flew to his wardrobe and pulled out his coat.

Tabitha watched him with her shining blue eyes. "Will you take me flying tonight?"

"Not tonight. I'm going to assess the situation over on the east side."

Tabitha leapt up from the chair, and the cat hopped to the floor. It eyed her indignantly. The girl looked around, as if someone would hear her, and asked in a harsh whisper, "Where the robberies are happening?"

He shrugged and buttoned his coat. "You were so worried about them, and it got me thinking. Those folks won't get much attention from the authorities. They're too low in rank for anyone to really care. Unless Grandfather pays a call to the authorities on their behalf...but we both know he never will."

Tabitha rushed in front of him. "But the robbers could be armed. You could get hurt."

Gareth flew to the balcony doors. "I'll be fine."

"You can't out fly a bullet."

He shrugged. "It's dark."

Her voice rose, and she no longer spoke in a whisper. "How would you come home and explain a bullet wound to Lord Pensees? Or what if someone saw you and told?"

Gareth stopped and bit his lip. She was right; he shouldn't risk it.

Tabitha's face lit up. "I have an idea."

She ran to the door, stepping over the cat. The orange tabby darted under his bed. She stepped out into the hall and peeked back in with a mischievous smile. "All's clear. Follow me."

Gareth threw up his hands but relented. When they reached the door to the attic, he had to ask her. "Where are we going?"

"I told you. I have an idea."

They reached the top of the attic stairs, Gareth reining in his flying pace to wait for Tabitha. She rushed over to a corner and pulled a sheet off a suit of armor. "You could wear this."

Gareth parked himself on top of an old wardrobe. He laughed. "I'm not wearing that."

"Why not? You'd be bullet proof. No one would recognize you. And if anyone sees you, no one's going to believe a story about a flying knight."

Gareth shook his head, but a smile formed on his lips. She might have something. She usually did. Tabitha was the smartest person Gareth knew, even if she were a girl. All the ladies he'd ever met bored him within minutes of a conversation's beginning. Perhaps it was being trapped in the chair and on the country estate that made Gareth long for conversation that went beyond the current fashion and silly giggles. It was another reason to swear off the idea of matrimony.

But Tabitha would need to marry well. Grandfather discouraged her in flaunting her intelligence. Gareth had to agree. Most gentlemen were stupid and only interested in cards and all things trivial. No mindless gentleman would want a wife who was so obviously his intellectual superior. Her origins and sharp mind were two strikes against her. But she was pretty and sweet-natured. Some man would be able to see past the other issues.

Gareth flew down from where he'd perched and picked up the sword that went with the suit. The tarnished blade felt heavy and awkward. Mr. Strong had been teaching him fencing as best he could with Gareth in a chair. He'd said it was part of a proper and well-rounded education. Gareth hadn't paid much attention, thinking swordplay a foolish endeavor for a cripple.

Perhaps just holding the sword would be enough to frighten criminals away. He surveyed the suit again and turned to Tabitha.

"Help me put it on over my clothes."

***

Gareth made his way to the east side of the village, slower than usual due to the extra weight. The armor's visor kept falling over his eyes, making visibility difficult. Sweat beaded on his forehead in the stifling lack of airflow.

At his rate of flight, it still didn't take long to reach the other side of town. He flew over one farm and saw nothing out of order. He did the same over at the Miller place. He'd been there with Sarah to get apples as a child. Nothing.

Just as he was about to give up, three young men came out of a shed, carrying tools. Gareth had never confronted anyone before, not really. He'd been surly to the help and to his grandfather all his life, but that was different.

He landed in the midst of them. They were around his age, but he didn't recognize any of them from church or the dinner parties he attended at Greenview.

"Put them back." Gareth deepened his voice to sound older and pointed with the sword.

The boys froze; their jaws dropped and eyes widened.

"I said, Put. Them. Back." His tone was controlled but with true power.

The tallest, a thin boy, backed away, tripping over a red-haired boy who had frozen in place. The tall one's tweed cap flew from his head, and he let out a sharp cry as he fell on his backside. He scrambled to his feet, snatched his cap, and sprinted down the lane.

"I said, PUT. THEM. BACK." Gareth's voice echoed through the suit, and he wondered if it boomed as loud outside of it.

The stocky boy holding the tools shook his head vigorously and whimpered. His wide eyes shone in the moonlight, and he suddenly looked younger than Gareth had thought at first. In desperation, the boy tried handing the bundle to the frozen boy, but they fell at his feet. With a cry of frustration, he picked the tools back up and tried to give them to the boy again, but they fell once more. He shrugged and bolted after the first boy.

Blinking hard, the frozen one seemed to realize he stood alone. His nose crinkled, joining the freckles, and his eyes looked black. He backed away, picking up speed with each step. He stepped into an irrigation ditch on the side of the road and fell into the mud. His dark eyes never left Gareth as he fumbled to his feet and started running backwards again. He fell twice more.

Gareth rolled his eyes in exasperation. "Oh, at least turn around and watch where you're going."

The boy nodded in agreement, eyes still wide. "Yes, right." And then took the advice by turning and tearing after his friends. The boy's backside was covered in brown mud, and Gareth chuckled.

He glanced at the scattered tools at his feet and considered picking them up. The armor would rattle and bump into something and probably get him caught. He shook his head. That would never do. At least the owner would find them in his yard and not gone.

***

When Gareth got home, he flew to Tabitha's balcony instead of his own. The orange cat sat there, looking out as if waiting for him. It followed him into Tabitha's room where his aunt lay on her bed with a book. The mutt was tucked into her side. She glanced up when he pushed open her doors.

"Did you find anything?" She jumped up and ran to him.

"Yes. I stopped some boys from taking tools at the Martin place."

"Did they see you? Did you have to fight them?"

Gareth placed the helmet on a table in the corner and began removing the rest. The cool air licked the sweat away and made him feel instant relief. "Yes, they saw me, but I didn't have to fight them."

Tabitha helped him out of the armor. "I bet they were scared to death when they saw you."

Gareth laughed. "They were. All three of them ran."

"Still, be careful. At some point, someone's going to challenge you with either a fist or a gun. Not everyone will run from a flying knight."

"I have my sword. Now that I have a reason to learn fencing, I'll take my practice with Mr. Strong seriously."

When he bent to pull off a metal legging, the blue stone fell from his waistcoat, and he caught it. His eyes darted to Tabitha who didn't seem to notice his secret treasure. The blue stone had lost the smell of flowers long ago, but it had become his good-luck charm whenever he flew out. Now he needed that sort of thing more than ever before.

***

Gareth wheeled himself to Mr. Strong's a half hour earlier than usual. He wanted to work more with the sword. He had pushed his way up the ramp to the door of Strong's cottage when Sarah came out, tugging her cardigan over her arms.

"Oh, Lord Smyth!" Sarah's worried green eyes were huge before she dropped her gaze to her rumpled skirt and began smoothing out the wrinkles. Her hands fluttered to her long, red hair. It hung loose about her shoulders which was uncommon. She pulled pins from it and stuck them in her teeth before scooping her hair up with both hands, twisting it into a hasty bun, and fastening it with the pins from her mouth. "Yer early."

Gareth narrowed his eyes. "What are you doing here?"

Sarah blinked several times as she bit her lip. "I came to deliver some laundry to Mr. Strong and tidy up a bit."

Gareth narrowed his eyes. "You're working for Mr. Strong, too?"

"Well, after yer grandfather had to cut me pay…"

Heat rose to Gareth's cheeks. Talking about the family's financial problems wasn't polite. "Yes, well, I came early to work on some numbers a little more."

"Numbers? Yes. Well. Have at it. I'll see ye later at yer grandfather's. Best knock before entering, since yer early." Sarah turned on her heel and left in haste.

Gareth knocked on the door three times as was his habit.

"Enter," a shaking voice called through the door.

Gareth turned the knob, pushed the door open, and wheeled himself in. He liked how Mr. Strong didn't rush to assist him but left it to him to do things on his own.

"Lord Smyth, you're early."

Gareth wheeled himself behind the door so he could push it shut. "Yes, I wanted some extra time to work on our fencing."

The old man nodded. "I see. Why the sudden interest? I've been trying to teach you fencing for months but you've shown no interest before."

Gareth composed himself and drew upon his typical expression of boredom. "I just feel that it's about time I learned every aspect of becoming a lord."

Mr. Strong made his way to a bureau and pulled out a long, slender sword by the hilt. "Let's start with a rapier." He tossed it toward Gareth.

Gareth instinctively reached out and grabbed it by the handle without a thought.

Mr. Strong let out a whistle. "Fine work, Lord Gareth. Ye might na be able to learn the footwork, but yer hands certainly be na crippled."

Gareth tilted his head to the side, trying to figure out the change in his tutor's accent.

Mr. Strong must have noticed his strange expression. "Oh, I studied fencing in Scotland. When I practice it, the old tongue comes back to me."

Gareth nodded and pushed himself out of his chair. He used his arms to help put one foot in front of the other for a wide stance. "It's true that I can't walk, but I can stand. Let's see how this goes in standing position."

Mr. Strong's eyes shone with delight as he smiled. "All right, let's go."

The tiny, old man placed his feet so that his body's side faced Gareth. Mr. Strong put one hand behind his back as he extended the sword with his other. "En garde!"

Gareth mimicked Mr. Strong's position as best he could and lifted his rapier at the shorter man. The two stared at each other for a moment. Adrenaline rose in Gareth's veins, and he tried his best to be sensitive to every possible move his tutor could make.

The grandfather clock in the entrance ticked slowly, each clockwork change clear. A waft of pine-scented cleaner rose from the floor, and he wondered for a moment if it would be slippery after Sarah's visit. While his thoughts had wandered, Mr. Strong launched his attack.

Gareth blocked Strong's blade with his own, the clanging of metal echoing in his ear as Mr. Strong pushed his blade hard against Gareth's sword. At least his tutor didn't hold back.

"You're strong for an old man," Gareth said before pushing off the sword and leaping back. He landed in a graceful stance similar to Mr. Strong's.

The tutor shook his head. "And you are quite lithe for a cripple."

Mr. Strong swung hard, and Gareth blocked him again. His tutor attacked with renewed fervor, and Gareth's feet slid back against the slick floorboards. With a smile, his tutor made a rounding motion with his blade and knocked Gareth's sword from his hand.

Gareth stared wide-eyed at the old man as he came at his chest full force with the tip of the rapier. Without thought, Gareth leapt to the side and hovered for a split second. *Dimwit.* He clenched his jaw and tried to cover his flying by landing to the side in a body roll, grabbing up his sword, and springing back to his feet.

"Well done." A wide grin spread across the old man's face. Mr. Strong placed the blade of the sword under his arm and began clapping. "Very nice indeed. You are truly growing into your abilities."

Gareth blinked at the old man. "You were coming at me full force. You could have killed me!"

The old man shook his head as he took Gareth's blade from him and headed for the cabinet. "No, I couldn't, because you jumped out of the way. I wanted to see how you would react with your life in danger, if you would let your natural instincts take over. And you did. Very good."

Gareth swallowed against his dry throat and tried to settle his pounding heart.

"Those were the small swords. Eventually we will work with these." Mr. Strong placed the rapiers in the bureau and pulled out a long, thick blade. The sword was longer than Mr. Strong, himself.

Gareth wondered how the old man could hold such a sword and how it had fit inside the cabinet.

"This is a Scottish highlander sword called a claymore. It is the sword of warriors and lairds and...kings." His eyes twinkled at the last word. Mr. Strong made his way to where Gareth stood. "Take hold of it and feel its strength and power."

Gareth took hold of the sword. It was heavy as he held it out and felt its balance. "How do you fight with such a large blade?"

"Simple. You make sure your sword is slicing through your enemy before theirs is slicing through you."

Gareth stared at his teacher.

Mr. Strong took the blade from Gareth and headed back toward the cabinet. "We will work with it eventually, after you've mastered the rapier and strengthened your upper body. Though I imagine pushing your chair has done a great deal for you."

"Speaking of my chair, could you please wheel it toward me?"

"It's obvious from our fight you could get to it yourself." The man continued to maneuver items in the cabinet.

Gareth glared at the old man's back. He couldn't fly now; the man could turn to him any moment. "But I'd have to jump there."

"So?"

"It's not dignified."

Strong shrugged, closed the cabinet, and faced him. "Never be embarrassed about what you have to modify in order to function. I like your independent spirit. It will do you well. Your pride, on the other hand, is your greatest weakness and we need to get rid of it as soon as possible. Go to your chair the best you can."

Gareth narrowed his eyes at the man. He crossed his arms, stiffened his spine, and waited for him to bring his chair.

Strong leaned against the cabinet doors. "I'm really not going to bring your chair to you. Don't be ashamed. You were quite agile during swordplay. Just do the same back to your chair."

Instinct led Gareth during the swordfight, but now he had returned to his faculties. How must he have looked as he jumped and hobbled about the room? He'd not give the tutor another display. He huffed. "Bring me my chair. That's an order, and last I checked you were under my grandfather's authority and so under mine. You don't order me; I order you."

Mr. Strong sighed and lifted his hands in a gesture. "I suppose we are at an impasse. I'll not do it."

The clock began the chime for the hour with the two men staring at each other. The tutor's expression remained unchanged. His face held the same bored expression that Gareth constantly strove for. But one better. The man never broke eye contact and smirked throughout.

When the clock's chimes had finished, Gareth swallowed his pride and dropped his eyes. He hobbled and jumped his way to the chair. Heat rose on his neck, and he'd never felt so demoralized. He placed his lap blanket across his legs and started pushing himself toward the door.

"Where are you going? We've not started your instruction for the day."

Gareth didn't turn to face the man. He didn't like being pressured to jump to his chair like some undignified wiggle worm. How could the old man say pride was Gareth's greatest weakness? It wasn't his pride. It was the stupid chair and his blasted legs that were his greatest weakness. Why couldn't he will them to step and walk? It was obvious they were strong enough to support him. It wasn't the old man's place to embarrass him or tell him he needed to get over it.

He opened the door and rolled down the ramp.

"Lord Smyth!" Strong called from the doorway. "When you are over your ire, you need to return for further instruction or else you'll never learn the claymore."

Chapter Three

7 Years Later

Gareth sat in the shade of the backyard, avoiding the sun and the scrutiny of the guests. Grandfather never hosted these sorts of gatherings and had always declined invitations. But now, he'd even hired a house staff for the day. Young ladies and gentlemen entertained themselves in his backyard. Some played badminton on the lawn, others sat at a card table.

Tabitha's cheeks were pink from running the badminton court. She shrieked and giggled as she hugged a dark-haired girl to keep from tripping. Both wore fashionable, white, corseted day dresses and hats.

Grandfather had noticed Tabitha wasn't being invited out into society enough to find a gentleman, so now society was invited to visit her. A last ditch effort to marry her off.

The game broke up and the other team left the net. The dark-haired girl hugged Tabitha again and peered up at Gareth under thick, dark lashes. He thought for a minute she grinned at him. He ignored the idea, knowing better. The girls stepped away from the net and under the shade of a tree.

***

Jessamine whispered into the ear of her new found friend, "Who is the young man in the shade there? The one watching us?"

Tabitha glanced in the direction Jessamine nodded. "Oh that is Lord Smyth, Lord Pensees's grandson."

"So, he's always lived in this shire?"

"Yes."

"Lord? That means he holds a title?" Jessamine bit her lip as she took in the handsome young man. His honey-blond hair was short and stylish for the times. It was hard to tell with him sitting, but he looked tall even still. His white shirtsleeves were pushed up, revealing muscular forearms.

"He doesn't hold a true title yet. He will inherit the title, Earl of Pensees. Being the next in line to someone of top rank, he gets the courtesy title of Lord until the Earl passes his title to his grandson." Tabitha pushed a strand of blonde hair that had escaped her ribbon, taking a glass of lemonade from a servant as they took a short break from the game.

Jessamine took a glass, too. "So much to remember with English etiquette and proper titles. In America, the only lord we have is the Good Lord. Would you mind introducing me?"

Tabitha returned her glass to the servant's tray. "I don't mind, but he will. Gareth hates introductions. He usually skips these things all together."

Jessamine returned her glass as well and glanced at the handsome young man. "Then why didn't he skip today?"

"Because it's my birthday, and he knew if he didn't come, it would disappoint me. He tries very hard not to do that."

"What if we made the introduction unavoidable? Then he wouldn't be irritated with you for introducing us."

"How would we make it unavoidable?"

"I have an idea."

***

Gareth watched the dark-haired girl pull away and motioned for Tabitha to move to the other side of the net.

The girl was quite pretty, Gareth couldn't help but notice, as they volleyed the birdie back and forth. He let his eyes linger over her form longer than normal. He chided himself. No young lady wanted to be settled with a cripple for a husband unless she was only interested in his title. He could never suffer such shallowness in a woman.

The dark-haired girl gave what looked like a nod to Tabitha who got a gleam in her eye and hit the shuttlecock with unnecessary force. Gareth wondered what they were up to when he noticed the birdie heading straight for him. The dark-haired girl ran backwards, trying to hit the thing, completely oblivious to Gareth directly in her path. Before he could move his chair out of her way, the girl tripped and landed squarely in his lap.

Large, brown eyes returned his stare. She covered her mouth and giggled. "I'm so sorry." She wiggled around in his lap, twisting until she gained her footing to stand.

Gareth pushed her up to assist her and to keep from embarrassing himself.

She backed away, and a red blush rose under her olive skin. "Again, sir, my apologies." Her accent was clearly American.

Gareth scowled back at her, adjusting his lap blanket. "You should watch where you're going, miss."

Tabitha ran up to join them. "Gareth, are you all right?" She glanced over at her friend whose eyes were also wide. There was something said in that look which Gareth wasn't sure about.

"Yes, yes, I'm fine." He winced at his tone. His answer was more cutting than his normal tone with Tabitha. It was the way he addressed everyone but her. Still, she wasn't fazed by it.

"Gareth, let me introduce you." Tabitha gestured to the pretty, dark-haired girl. "This is Miss Jessamine Cardinal Keller. She and her father are visiting from the United States."

Then she gestured to Gareth. "And this is Lord Tristan Gareth Smyth, future Earl of Pensees. His grandfather is my guardian and benefactor."

Jessamine made a quick curtsy. "Future Earl? Very nice to make your acquaintance." She glanced up under long lashes and smiled.

Gareth waved her off. "Yes, yes. Nice to make yours. Try to be more careful in the future."

Her grin widened as she peeked over at Tabitha. "Yes, of course. My apologies for landing in your lap like that."

Gareth's pulse raced just a bit. He motioned again for them to be off. He wasn't accustomed to young ladies paying him attention, much less sitting in his lap. He didn't wish to embarrass the girls or himself with the effect she had on him.

The girls finally scurried off, to Gareth's relief. But wherever they were in the yard, the girl Jessamine would glance over at him and smile sweetly. Gareth in turn would adjust his lap blanket and look away, trying to forget the sweet scent which had lingered in his personal space after she had left it.

***

The afternoon meal was taken outside as a picnic, with everyone sitting on blankets under the tree. Gareth was

51

not interested in staying. He wasn't *that* hungry. Tabitha sat on the blanket next to his chair, and he snatched his opportunity.

"Tabitha, I'd like to excuse myself. I'm feeling fatigued and need a nap," Gareth pleaded with his young aunt. He didn't enjoy dining picnic style out among the flies any more than he enjoyed dining among society. He felt he'd suffered long enough, watching everyone play games and chatter all morning.

He'd expected her to relent, but instead she grabbed his arm and pouted. "Oh, not yet. I've not cut my cake. Stay just a little longer."

Gareth closed his eyes and sighed. "Fine. But just until lunch is over, and we cut the cake. You know I don't enjoy these gatherings."

Tabitha squealed. "Tell me what you'd like to eat, and I'll get it for you."

He told her, and she went to make him a plate. He watched her go and hoped his torture would be over quickly. In her absence, Jessamine took a seat on the blanket next to him. His heart raced as he watched her from the corner of his eye. But he refused to turn his head. Instead, he watched the other gentlemen and ladies settle on blankets nearby as if he found it of interest.

Jessamine finally broke the silence. Her voice was light and had a musical tone as she spoke quietly. "My father and I have been hearing stories about your little town. It seems you have a medieval ghost protecting your shire."

Gareth turned and peered down at the girl. "Pardon?"

Her large, brown eyes never faltered. She sat up on her knees, biting her lip in expectation. "The Flying Knight. What do you think about the local legend—have you ever seen him?"

Gareth looked away. "Rubbish."

"So you don't believe in him?" There was doubt in her tone.

Gareth turned back to face her. "Is that why you've come here from America, to find this flying knight?"

She grinned. "Maybe. My father has plans to marry me to some stuffy English lord. But I think marrying a flying knight would be much more exciting. What do you think?"

Gareth looked away. "I'm not sure a ghost would have need of a wife."

Tabitha finally returned with his plate. He snatched it and said, "Yes, please give me my food so I can fulfill my promise and leave this ridiculous party."

The two girls smiled and glanced at each other before scurrying off, whispering as they headed for the food together. They returned before Gareth had finished his plate. He ate in silence as the girls continued their chatter. He tried to ignore the irritating American girl but found it difficult. She wasn't the normal pale, English young lady he was accustomed to. Jessamine was a little more olive toned and more than a little pretty, especially when she smiled at him, which she kept doing every time he peered in her direction.

Jessamine reached out and took hold of Tabitha's charm bracelet. "I love this. It's very beautiful."

Tabitha fingered her abacus charm. "Thank you."

Jessamine reached into the collar of her dress and pulled out a chain. "I have a similar necklace."

Many of the charms in the cluster matched, the owl, the heart, and the clock, but Jessamine had a wing instead of abacus. Again the two girls exchanged a knowing look. Jessamine's grin grew wider. "A BUBO. I knew there was a reason I felt a kinship with you the moment we met. My mother gave me mine. May I ask where you got yours?"

Tabitha glanced about as she spoke in a very cautious manner. "I got it at my *bonnet* club."

Jessamine's eyebrows raised. "Bonnet club?"

"Yes, several ladies here in the shire meet once a week. It includes women from among all the classes and ages, even as far away as Ardenshire. We take our old ...*bonnets* and we...rework them into something more...*modern*."

Jessamine smiled. "I see. So you take outdated...*bonnets* you have around the house and modernize them."

"Yes. I have a whole room dedicated to my..." Tabitha glanced around. "...bonnets. Some of the ladies have designed all new original bonnets. I've never seen the like of them. We have several talented members in our *bonnet* club."

Jessamine glanced up at Gareth. "Lord Smyth, have you seen her bonnets? Do you approve?"

Gareth let out a sigh. "Why the devil would I care about ladies' bonnets?" He turned and glowered at Tabitha. "I'm going in."

"We still haven't had cake," Tabitha pleaded.

"Save me a piece for later." He handed his plate to Tabitha and started pushing his wheels.

"I'll push you in." Jessamine jumped up and took hold of the back of the chair.

"No, I can take myself in."

"I really don't mind. Consider it my penance for falling all over you. Besides, maybe Tabitha could show me her bonnet room?"

Tabitha leapt up from her spot on the blanket. "Yes, of course. I'd love to."

Gareth crossed his arms and slouched in his chair. With Jessamine there, he'd have to wait for a servant to carry him up the stairs. He glanced back at her and noticed she was examining his chair as she pushed it. Her eyes perused the thing from top to bottom and then at Gareth. It made him even more self conscious than normal.

"Do you have a problem with my chair?"

Jessamine blinked hard, a surprised look on her face. "I was just wondering why Tabitha hasn't made it a bonnet project. It would be very easy to do."

"Stop!"

Tabitha stepped in front of Gareth. "Is something wrong?"

"Yes. There is nothing wrong with my chair. It does not need ribbons and flowers like Tabitha's remade bonnets. You are getting on my last nerve. Run along to the bonnet room. I'll take myself the rest of the way in."

"Are you sure? I don't mind pushing you." Jessamine bent around from behind Gareth to ask. He caught a whiff of her floral scent. It muddled his brain for a second before he answered. "Go! Just go."

The girls made their way into the manor. He overheard Jessamine ask, "Is he always so grumpy?"

Tabitha answered, "Only on the days ending in 'Y'."

They both giggled and scurried away.

With a sigh, Gareth pushed his wheels, heading for the foyer. He was just about to fly up the stairs when he heard laughter from above. They were probably still laughing at him and his inability to socialize the way other young men his age could, laying on false charm to attract the pretty ladies.

The thought of remaining in the house with them down the hall repulsed him. He spun his chair around and headed for the kitchen exit in order to avoid the other guests. The halls were empty as the staff would be out tending the crowd.

He would go visit Mr. Strong. The old man was no longer his tutor, but Gareth often visited him for swordplay.

Gareth entered the kitchen and halted when he saw Sarah with her head bent over the table, face in hands. Her breath caught between sobs. Gareth froze. He had no idea how to handle emotional moments. The idea of backing out of the kitchen appealed to him, but he was afraid any movement might rouse the weeping woman.

Sarah lifted her eyes, and they met his. She leapt to her feet and wiped her eyes with her shirtsleeve. "Oh, Mr. Gareth. Do ye be needin' something?"

Gareth shook his head. "No, I…" caught off guard, he temporarily forgot where he was headed. "I'm off to visit Mr. Strong."

"Today?"

"Of course today." Gareth glowered and wheeled himself past her toward the door.

"Will he be expectin' ye?"

"Yes." The lie burned on his tongue as usual. He swallowed and felt sick. Lies always did that to him. Even small ones. "I'll be back later this afternoon."

Sarah curtseyed. "Aye, m'lord."

He was halfway down the lane when he heard the kitchen door slam. He glanced back to see Sarah running full speed toward the stable. He shook his head at her odd behavior, and then he remembered her tears. Perhaps she and Thompton were fighting. That was probably it. All those years of acting happy and loving. No married people could be so happy all the time.

Gareth made his way to Mr. Strong's. He hated when he had to wheel himself instead of fly, but he couldn't risk being seen in daylight. People in town knew him.

The townspeople glanced his way and ignored him, as they always did when his grandfather wasn't around. He wondered if they would continue to treat him so nonchalantly when he became the Earl of Pensees and owned half the shire.

At Mr. Strong's door, Gareth pushed himself up the ramp and knocked his usual three raps. At first there was no answer. When he lifted his hand to knock again, he heard a slam from the back of the house. He leaned in and listened harder as booted feet stomped toward the door. Mr. Strong yanked it open and stood, panting.

"Ah, Lord Smyth, what a nice surprise." The old man held the door open and motioned with his arm. "Please come in."

Gareth pushed himself into the foyer and turned to face the man. His eyes looked red and puffy. "Are you unwell?"

The old man reached into his pocket, pulled out a handkerchief, and rubbed at his eyes. "I'm well. Just received bad news today. A very old and beloved friend passed on."

"Oh, I'm sorry to hear it."

"It wasn't totally unexpected. Sorrow brings death early to some. He'd known too much of it in the last of his years."

Gareth motioned for the door. "I can leave and come another time."

The old man shook his head. "Nonsense. Your leaving won't bring him back. We must move on and get the next generation ready to take over for the last. You're here for swordplay?"

Gareth nodded. "Yes, it helps settle my nerves."

Mr. Strong headed for the cupboard. "Rapier or claymore?"

"Claymore. It's more exhausting."

The old man tossed the long blade to Gareth who caught it easily by the hilt. Bearing the full weight of it in one hand forced his arm muscles to flex.

"Oh, ye want to work up a sweat and forget everything but the fight, do ye? Must be a lady involved." He laughed and rolled up his sleeves.

Gareth noticed a slight change in Mr. Strong's accent. "Tabitha's got friends over. One in particular is quite irritating. Pretty but annoying."

The old man grinned as he took his position and Gareth leapt to his stance, away from his chair. Strong had won that argument long ago. If Gareth wanted to continue his swordplay, he'd have to get himself to and from his chair.

"Pretty and she gets under your skin? That's always the best combination. Makes life exciting."

Gareth shook his head. "No, it just makes it annoying." He leapt forward, raised the claymore high above his head, and brought it down hard over Mr. Strong. The old man ducked and blocked Gareth's blow with his own sword, creating a loud clang. Strong pushed up with both hands and forced the sword away. Gareth jumped back, landing legs apart for balance.

"You've always amazed me, old man. Most aren't as strong." Gareth spun and swung the claymore with two hands, watching as his tutor adjusted and blocked him.

"Strong *is* my name." The old man laughed. He followed with his own attack which forced Gareth to his knees with his claymore overhead.

Gareth grunted and pushed the man away. "How old are you?"

"Older than I look." Mr. Strong charged at Gareth, letting out a guttural war cry, swinging the blade over his shoulder in a diagonal motion. Gareth retreated, eyes wide, working furiously to block and get out of the way of the attack. He found himself backed into a corner as Mr. Strong was bringing down a deathblow.

Gareth shot out to the side, between the old man's arms and legs, flying forward and low. He feared his speed had been too unnatural and tried to cover the flight by curling and rolling on the floor. He popped back up to a standing position. The old man's chest heaved in the same rhythm as his own. Gareth wiped the sweat from his forehead with his sleeve, brushing back the wet tendrils against his head. "You take our play too seriously at times, old man. If I hadn't jumped out of your way, you could have killed me."

"When you find yourself in a real battle, it won't be play. I need to know you can handle it when your life is threatened for real."

"Who's going to attack a man in a wheelchair? He'd have to look at me first."

"There you go again, acting like your wheelchair keeps everyone out. It's not true, you know. It's you who pushes them away. The annoying, pretty thing that sent you here, I bet you pushed her away, too." The old man broke his stance and walked over to a table. He poured two glasses of water and carried one to Gareth.

Gareth shook his head and rested the claymore's point in the floorboards. He accepted the cup and drank it down before handing it back. "I didn't come here to discuss my love life with an old bachelor."

Mr. Strong turned and carried the glasses back to the table. "Whoever said I was a bachelor? And love life, you say. So you think you love the girl?"

Gareth shook his head in frustration before leaping to his chair and having a seat. "No, I don't love her. I don't even know her. I don't believe in that kind of love anyway. So if you aren't a bachelor, you're what? A widower?"

"No, I'm not a widower either. I'm happily married and have been for years."

Gareth looked down the hall and toward the kitchen. "Where's your wife?"

"She doesn't stay here. I'm only in town to work. I often visit her, and she comes to visit me. And what kind of love is it you don't believe in?"

"The kind that's supposed to last forever. The reason young people get all puppy-eyed and feel the need to bind themselves to someone for the rest of their lives. Only to grow bored and seek the companionship of another. Why bother to begin with?"

Mr. Strong pulled a seat from his desk over and sat across from Gareth. The old man frowned. "You are awfully jaded for a man so young."

"I speak what I see." He looked out the window at the patch of blue sky. He'd already opened up more than he liked.

"So what kind of love do you believe in?"

Gareth sat in silence thinking about it. "I care very much for Tabitha. I'd like to see her taken care of and happy. More than I care to be happy myself, I want it for her. So I believe in that kind of love."

Mr. Strong's wrinkled forehead scrunched as his brows furrowed. "Well, if that's how you feel about love and marriage, why force the whole thing on poor Tabitha? According to you, she's only going to be forgotten for another. You'd have her stuck in a loveless marriage? Better she becomes a governess, wouldn't it?"

"I...she..." Gareth couldn't think of an answer. Finally, he pursed his lips and glared at the old man. "I didn't come here to talk or to think. I came here to swordfight. If we are done with that—we are done." He tossed his sword to Mr. Strong who caught it in one hand. The muscles in his forearm bulged as he grasped it.

Gareth pushed himself to the door and forced himself down the ramp. How had his distracting game of swords turned into a talk on love? If love and marriage could only bring misery, why did he want it for Tabitha? Maybe he didn't think it was the way of all marriages but the way of most. He wanted Tabitha to be treasured by someone and protected and cared for. The way Thompton opened doors for Sarah and touched her cheek when he came to the kitchen. Maybe they were fighting today, but for the most part, they were the happiest married couple he'd ever seen.

He could picture that for Tabitha. She should have that life.

It just wasn't for him. He was the rejected, crippled heir. The forgotten and abandoned son of his mother. The man no one looked in the eye because they'd have to bend down to do it. No, he'd not find love, nor would he suffer some woman's pity in love's stead.

He pushed himself harder toward the house. He would claim he didn't feel well once home and have his tray sent to his room. Come darkness, he would have his freedom.

Chapter Four

Jessamine fidgeted with her necklace. "Are you sure it's okay for me to come to your BUBO club?"

She wasn't usually so nervous about meeting new people. The gentle rocking motion of the carriage made her a bit nauseated. At least the breeze wafted in and kept her from feeling stifled by the hot afternoon air.

Tabitha smiled and patted her hand. "They will welcome you with open arms. They always do. Mrs. Collins hosts the club meetings weekly. All women with a mind for automation are welcome, no matter their class. At least it's one thing I might be able to keep."

Tabitha's pretty smile was gone, replaced by a downcast look of worry.

Jessamine reached out and touched her shoulder. "Are you unwell?"

Tabitha's smile looked forced. "I'm fine…for now."

"And soon you won't be?"

"I have a habit of looking for numbers to figure. I like them. They comfort me, because it's one of the few things in life which are perfectly predictable. When I'm stressed or bored, I go through Lord Pensees's books and work them. Only, the numbers are not working out favorably." She frowned and shook her head, realizing she was speaking out of turn. "I'm sorry. I shouldn't be sharing Lord Gerald's personal matters with you. That wasn't becoming."

"You call him Lord Pensees *and* Lord Gerald?"

Tabitha blushed. "I'm not allowed a more personal term for him, like the way Gareth addresses him as Grandfather. But he allows me to use his Christian name in private with Lord preceding it."

"Are you related to the family?"

Tabitha answered Jessamine with only a stare.

"I'm sorry. I'm speaking out of turn this round. There are not so many social taboos in America."

"It's quite all right. I will answer you like this. When Henry VIII's mistress gave him a son, he wasn't allowed the surname of Tudor but given the surname Fitzroy, meaning son of royalty, as a way for the king to acknowledge him as his son. I am Tabitha Fitzgerald and am the legal ward of Lord Gerald Smyth, Earl of Pensees."

Understanding sunk in as Jessamine's eyes widened. "I see."

"Do you view me differently now?"

Jessamine reached over and patted her friend on the hand. "Nonsense. We are sisters in automation. The rest is unimportant."

"I wish everyone saw it as such. With no money or title, and the family estate in trouble, I will be seeking another situation shortly."

Jessamine's heart went out to Tabitha. She hardly knew her, and yet a fast bond had formed between them. "Is there anything I can do? Do you think your family would accept assistance from me or my father?"

Tabitha shook her head and stared out the window, but her eyes seemed to be looking at something other than the rolling scenery. "No, pride would never allow them to accept charity."

Jessamine leaned in to whisper, "If I were to marry Mr. Gareth, my money would be his money. And...you know why I'm here."

Tabitha rolled her sky-blue eyes. "Gareth will never marry. He won't even talk to a lady. He says he'd be bored with nothing polite to say after a five-minute conversation."

Jessamine laughed. "He considers his first five minutes of conversation to be polite?"

Tabitha laughed, too. "Gareth is sweet at heart. He really is. His grandfather and others, they've made him feel...I don't know, self-conscious. He pushes everyone away except me. Neither of us have mothers, so we bonded early."

The carriage stopped, and Thompton opened the door for them. Jessamine smiled at him. "Thank you, Thompton."

He bowed and tilted his head toward Tabitha. "What time should I be back fer ye?"

"You don't need to return. Mrs. Collins will see us home."

Thompton nodded, climbed back up, and drove the carriage on. Tabitha grabbed Jessamine's arm and looped hers through it. "Now we go around back to the stables."

A dark cloud hovered almost directly over the stable. It nearly blocked out the sun and seemed strange in the otherwise clear sky. Two women stood in front of the building, each in the other's personal space and both red faced as they argued.

A stern lady dressed in black and a high collar crossed her arms in front of her chest. "We've told you, the BUBO club is not a good fit for your sort of automation. You are no longer welcome to our meetings."

Jessamine shot a glance at Tabitha, whose face fell. Tabitha whispered, "That's Mrs. Williams."

The other stringy-haired woman stood back, placing her hands on each side of her primrose bustle. Her mouth twisted in derision. "Do you really think women can gain acceptance in society except by force?"

Mrs. Williams pointed away from the stables. "You are not welcome, Mrs. Steel."

The dark-haired woman gathered up her skirts and stormed in their direction. Tabitha pulled Jessamine to the side and out of sight. They waited until the woman had stormed by before approaching the door. Jessamine's stomach twisted as they stepped toward Mrs. Williams. The woman's lips were puckered, and she ran her hands on both sides of her severe, ash-blonde bun. She stood much taller than Jessamine or Tabitha.

Mrs. Willimams blinked hard and nodded to Tabitha. "Miss Fitzgerald, nice to see you. And who is your guest?"

Tabitha pulled Jessamine in closer. "This is Miss Jessamine Keller. She's visiting from the Americas."

The woman narrowed her eyes at Jessamine. "And do you already know how to re-work hats?"

Jessamine reached into her collar and pulled out her owl pendant. "Yes, my mother taught me."

"And your inventions…are they items to improve life or take it?"

Jessamine's hand flew to her chest as she glanced toward Tabitha in shock. "Improve life, of course."

The woman's face softened. "I'm sorry, I had to ask after a recent incident. Welcome. I'm Mrs. Williams. I've got door duty this week. Go on in and make yourself comfortable at one of our many work stations."

Jessamine followed Tabitha into the stables as Mrs. Williams held the door open. The stable was large inside and had been converted into a work shed. One group of ladies in smocks crowded around a buggy. It was like some of the automobiles she'd seen in South Carolina.

The lady wearing brown knickerbockers, a puffy sleeved shirt, and a leather apron stood by it, speaking to those gathered around. "This is my version of the automobile, but without the smelly exhaust from gasoline. Instead, it is hydro-powered. If you look right here, you will find my faux river. A spooning mechanism pivots and causes the water to rush forward, pushing the tiny waterwheels. In turn, they push the gears causing the wheels to turn. A tank catches the water as it flows. When the tank hits empty, you simply pull over, take the jug the water has emptied into and refill the tank at upper mouth of the faux river. It's clean, and you can even keep fish in the tanks." She lifted up one of the tanks to show goldfish swimming about. "Just remember to feed them." She dropped bits of food in the water.

The crowd around her clapped and cheered.

Jessamine and Tabitha made their way to another display. A young woman with orange hair, wearing tattered, canvas pants, stood by what looked like a barrel on wagon wheels.

"As many of you know, my father is a farmer. Every year I walk behind him, dropping seeds as he plows, and cover the seeds with my foot as I go. All day long, every day, until planting is done. I've spent years toiling, and my mind spun around in my head trying to think of a way to make it more efficient. Now, I've come up with this planter."

She walked around to the side of the barrel. "You take the crank and turn it around over and over until it won't turn anymore. This winds up the cord. Once you do that, you wheel it to the ground you want planted. The plow up front digs the trench while this belt pushes seeds out about a foot apart. This flap on the back covers the seed with just the right amount of dirt. And there's even a spout at the rear to water as it goes. Cuts the planting time in half and requires fewer hands."

A grey-haired woman stepped out and started the applause. Tabitha leaned in and whispered, "That's Mrs. Collins."

Mrs. Collins waited for the clapping to stop before she spoke. "This is why we are here. We are women with minds for automation. God did not intend us to rot in a corner with them. When God created man, He saw that the man needed a helper and created a woman. Now, the God I serve is a smart God with grand ideas. How smart would it be to offer an idiot as a helper? To say, 'Here you go. She's not really good for much. She's kind of entertaining when naked but other than that, put her in a safe place so she doesn't hurt herself.' No, that would make no sense at all."

The woman's warm eyes glowed as she addressed them. "We are not trying to take over the work of men. We

71

only wish to be included. We see things from a different perspective than the men, and that's a good thing. It is my hope that, one day, women and men can work side by side and forge new technologies together."

When she finished, the crowd applauded and began to separate into groups to discuss projects. Mrs. Collins approached Tabitha. "Miss Fitzgerald, so nice to see you. May I be introduced to your friend?"

Tabitha bowed in reverence to the woman. Obvious admiration and respect shone from her as she watched the older woman from under long, dark lashes. "This is Miss Jessamine Keller. Her mother is responsible for automating textile factories throughout the southeastern United States."

The woman faced Jessamine with a welcoming grin. "Your mother is an automator?"

"Yes, my father has a great head for business and my mother has one for mechanics. Together they've built an empire and improved working conditions. They have their home office in a town called Chesnee in South Carolina. Their automations have freed up children from the factories. She's developed an innovative fabric blend that will change the world of textiles, as well as the military."

Mrs. Williams stepped closer. "I thought you said your inventions were to improve life and not take it."

Jessamine nodded her head. "Yes, quite right. But when a woman's son finds himself at war, would his mother not have him shielded from the danger around him? My mother has designed a fabric as soft as cotton but as tough as armor."

"That is amazing dear." Mrs. Collins grasped her by the forearm and nodded. "I applaud all your mother is doing on both fronts. I wish someone would take up the cause of the children here. Many children have suffered in factories for their cheap labor, casting education aside. It's a terrible affliction."

Jessamine nodded. "My parents have also endowed schools in Chesnee so that the populace will be educated and ready for a future in automation. They don't want an ignorant workforce."

"And are the girls educated along with the boys?"

A warm smile crossed Jessamine's face as she thought of what her parents were doing. "Yes, ma'am. Girls and boys are educated together."

"Wonderful. Now, has Tabitha taken you to see what she's been working on?"

Jessamine shook her head. "Not yet."

Mrs. Collins gestured for them to lead the way. "Please Tabitha, introduce us to your automation."

Tabitha led them to a countertop full of appliances. "I've spent a great deal of time in the kitchen at home with Sarah, our housekeeper. Watching her work has helped me come up with great ideas for how to automate her labors. Automation should be for the common woman, too."

She pointed to a device on a shelf. "This simple flame under this steel barrel works to keep water heated at all times. No need to boil for tea or dishwashing. This coil also feeds from the flame to this metal box and is ready for small things like reheating a meal for lunch or for toasting bread.

"And I've added springs to push the door open and the rack out once the desired temperature is reached. It triggers this bell and lets the person who is cooking it know it is done."

Jessamine tipped at her hat in salute to her friend. "Very smart indeed."

Mrs. Collins turned her attention to Jessamine. "Miss Keller, did you bring anything to display?"

Jessamine grinned in anticipation. Her heart raced as she thought of finally sharing what she had been working on. "Why yes, I did."

Chapter Five

"Jessamine and her father have been invited to stay at the manor," Tabitha told Gareth after dinner.

"What? And now I'm to listen to the two of you laugh at me all day *and* all night, too?" Gareth flew to the other side of his bedroom and looked out the balcony door. He always did when he felt trapped.

"We don't laugh at you."

"I heard the two of you."

"You heard us laugh but not at you. Really, you should know me better than that."

Gareth eyed his young aunt. "I do know you. It's her I don't know."

"Their staying here will remedy that."

"I don't wish it remedied. How will they stay? The house hasn't held a guest in years. We only have Thompton and Sarah."

"Lord Gerald has hired more staff for the visit. Besides, they're American. They have no clue if what we do at dinner is proper or not."

Gareth flew to his trunk and got out his suit of armor. "So we are going deeper into debt to impress ignorant Yanks? Wonderful. Go on to bed and let me dress. I'm going out."

As she headed for the door, Tabitha shot him a hurt, slightly angry look.

It pierced Gareth in the heart, and he felt guilty for a moment, but the feeling fled the moment she closed the door. He'd have his freedom, even if just for now.

***

The next morning, servants carried in steamer trunks while Sarah directed everyone where to put things. Disgusted with what he saw in the foyer, Gareth retreated to his room. They never had house guests. And now, with the house fully staffed, how was he to fly about as he liked? He'd be stuck in the blasted chair for the whole visit.

Gareth took to flying back and forth in his room, pacing from wall to wall, and dreaded the week ahead with guests. A knock sounded at his door. He came down and settled himself in the wingchair. "Yes?"

Sarah entered. "A package just arrived fer ye, sir."

76

She moved out of the way while her husband, Thompton, carried in a long wooden crate.

"Just place it on his bed, Sweeting," she said, gesturing.

Gareth averted his eyes, pretending not to notice Sarah pat her husband's behind. The two were always like that, touching and calling each other pet names. Thompton placed the long crate on the burgundy quilt, and it took up nearly the length of it from headboard to foot. A white pine box with hardly a mark on it and no return address. Thompton nodded, took out a crowbar, and cracked open the top. He left the lid down and bowed in Gareth's direction before turning to leave.

"Would ye like me to have Thompton bring up yer chair so you can get to yer package?"

"No, I can manage. Please close the door as you leave."

Sarah nodded and curtsied before withdrawing.

The moment the door clicked shut, Gareth flew to the bed and lifted the lid of the crate. He pushed away packing straw to reveal a long sword. Gareth lifted the flat blade with an edge on both sides and inspected it. It was a Scottish claymore. The hilt was ornate, with the wooden handle carved to look like vines intertwined together. There was something familiar to Gareth about the look of the vines but he couldn't think of what they reminded him.

Another knock came from his door.

Gareth sat on his bed, still holding and inspecting the sword. "Yes?"

Tabitha stuck her head around the door. "Can we come in?"

Before he could give an answer, she and Jessamine rushed into his room. Tabitha's blue eyes grew large as she took in the claymore. "Where did you get that?"

Jessamine eyed the sword from top to bottom. "It's beautiful."

Mr. Strong, he thought. But without a return address, Gareth couldn't be certain. Instead, he shook his head as he lifted it, still inspecting the blade. "I'm not sure where it came from. Sarah said it just arrived for me."

Tabitha held out a big, floppy, floral hat. "We are off to my bonnet club. Should Lord Pensees or Mr. Keller ask, tell them we will not be late for dinner."

He frowned. "Yes, I will tell them."

Tabitha turned to go, but Jessamine stepped closer, placing her hand on the hilt. "The vines are beautiful. I wonder if the Flying Knight wields a sword as grand as this."

Her hand brushed against Gareth's. He glanced over at her, taking in her knowing smile, one that made him question all she might know about him. Again he inhaled her scent. She was too close. It took all he had not to fly off the bed to the other side of the room and cower in a corner. He wasn't accustomed to such an onrush of feelings. Their newness made them more difficult to suppress. He would have to practice.

Jessamine smiled, and her large, brown eyes peered into his. "I look forward to dinner tonight with you and your family."

With a nod, she walked out the door. Tabitha shut it behind them.

***

Jessamine leaned against the wall once in the hall. Her heart pounded in her ears. It was him; she knew it. The eyes were the same and held the same intensity she remembered.

"Jessie, are you all right?" Tabitha made her way to where Jessamine had propped herself and placed her hand on Jessamine's forehead. "You seem unwell."

Jessamine took a deep breath and then let it out. "I'm fine. Just excited. It's finally going to happen. My father has spoken with Lord Pensees. It has all being arranged. I'm so glad you had this emergency bonnet club meeting called, or I should have paced the floor of my room in anticipation."

"We need to hurry. Mrs. Collins has just found out about a rally organized for suffragettes by Emmeline Pankhurst. She is a member of one of our sister bonnet clubs. We are making banners and printing pamphlets today."

Jessamine grabbed her friend's shoulder. "Women are asking for the vote? How exciting. We don't even have that in America. Let's go."

***

That evening, Tabitha knocked and entered Gareth's room around the same time she always did. Her blue, silk skirts rustled as she made her way to him. Gareth knew little of fashion, but it was obvious the dress was not with the current style. It had probably been made over at least three times now by Sarah and looked worn.

His loyal confidant. She had come to stand lookout for him so he could fly downstairs to his chair before dinner. He no longer allowed a male servant to carry him back and forth.

"Lord Gerald wishes you join him in his study before dinner."

Gareth frowned. "Does it not bother you to call him that?"

Tabitha plopped down into the wingchair. "He gave me the last name 'Fitzgerald,' so he acknowledges me that way. At least he didn't send me to an orphanage, and he's trying to secure my future. I assume all of that means he cares. He's not as harsh as when we were younger. I think poverty and old age has broken his pride down a bit. He speaks highly of you and your dealings with the locals on your business rides together."

"He does?" Gareth didn't know that. He glanced out the door. "You're sure your houseguest isn't around? Or one of the other servants?"

"Mr. Keller is outside checking out the stables with Thompton. Sarah has tied up all the house servants with dining room and dinner preparation. Jessamine, on the other hand, is busy in my bonnet room at the moment, working on something quite extensive. When she sets her mind to something, she becomes quite absorbed. I promise it's safe."

"How interesting can a bunch of reworked hats be?"

Tabitha grinned. "Maybe one day I'll show you some of my things. Jessamine's very impressed with my skills. She's even told her father."

"I saw the hats you two brought back. They looked exactly the same way they did when you left. They always do."

Tabitha only giggled. She opened the door, glided down the stairs in silence, and called out in a whisper, "All is clear."

Gareth flew down to his chair and took a seat. Tabitha wheeled him toward the study. She stepped around the chair to knock.

"Please be open to whatever he has to say. That's all I ask." She leaned in to kiss Gareth on the cheek and scooted away.

What was that about?

His grandfather's deep voice boomed from behind the oak door. "Enter."

Gareth swallowed hard, turned the knob, and pushed the door open to wheel himself in. His grandfather, Lord

Gerald Smyth, Earl of Pensees, faced the fireplace, holding a glass of amber liquid.

At first, the only sound was the crackle of the fire until Grandfather's voice interrupted the silence. "Gareth, would you like something from the bar?"

"No, sir, but thank you."

His grandfather turned to him, his face distraught. His color was that of paste, and the lines around his eyes had grown more pronounced. The old man's brows furrowed and then released as if he'd just accepted whatever terrible thought had possessed him. It was a look he had often these days.

"I need to discuss Tabitha's future with you. I know she's as dear to you as she is to me, and you've always taken it upon yourself to look out for her. Don't think I haven't noticed. I've admired that about you. Your father never thought of anyone but himself. I suppose your devotion must come from your mother's side." The old man looked away and took a quick gulp of his drink before he mumbled, "God knows you didn't learn it from me."

Gareth looked away and flared his nostrils in derision. *Some devotion, to go and abandon her child.*

His grandfather continued. "I'm counting on you to help me now. This isn't what I wanted for Tabitha or for you, but there isn't really any other choice."

Gareth felt his forehead wrinkle. "Grandfather, I'm not sure what you are talking about."

"We're out of money. Your father died with gambling debts that I've been paying off for years. The lands don't bring in the income they once did, and I've got nothing to offer a possible suitor to make him interested in Tabitha. I should have married her mother, and then she would at least have a family connection. But no, I was too proud to marry a servant. I didn't even know the depths of my feelings until they told me she'd died giving birth and handed me Tabitha." His grandfather faced him with tears in his eyes and finished the dregs of his glass.

Gareth sat in silence. He wasn't accustomed to such frank talk from his grandfather. "Sir, I…" he stopped, still not sure what to say.

"Mr. Keller is here visiting his sister in town, but he's also here to secure a future for his daughter. Miss Keller has become fond of Tabitha and has offered to let her go home with her father and be presented in American society in the hopes of finding a match for her there. They are new money, but they have lots of it. Miss Keller seeks to secure a good match here among the peerage. It should break down the door for them into high New York society where Tabitha will be presented."

Gareth sat up straight. *Tabitha leaving? America?* He'd never thought of her leaving England. "Does she want to go stay with the Kellers?"

"Very much. But there is one condition." Grandfather stared at the empty glass in his hand and rotated it so that it caught the light from the fireplace.

Gareth's forehead scrunched. "So we need to find a man of title willing to marry Miss Keller? You know I don't have close friends to suggest."

"No. Miss Keller has set her sights on you. The idea of becoming Lady Smyth, future Countess of Pensees, seems to suit her very much. They will take Tabitha and pay all the expenses and present her to American society, *if* you marry Miss Jessamine Keller."

Gareth's mouth fell open. "I'm to marry Miss Keller? I don't even like the girl."

Grandfather stared at the glass, but a smirk played on his lips. "It would seem she likes you."

Thoughts and possibilities ran through Gareth's jumbled mind. He couldn't have a wife. He'd have no freedom. He couldn't let her catch him flying. He'd forever be stuck in the blasted chair. His fingers clenched into fists while his heart fluttered in panic. "No, I won't do it. I can't."

Grandfather set his glass on the mantle fireplace, trudged over to his desk, and collapsed in his chair. He put his elbows on the desk and rested his face in his hands.

The clock on the mantle ticked, but Gareth's heart raced it and won. Grandfather finally sat up and gazed at Gareth. His look was somber. "I was afraid of this. I had hoped your loyalty to Tabitha would be enough. We have no money. This meal is the last I can afford to purchase as our credit is strapped. Tabitha will have to send out letters seeking employment as a governess, and we will lock ourselves up to starve, I suppose."

Gareth wheeled closer to his grandfather. "Things are really that desperate?"

The old man's sober, blue eyes glared back. "They are exactly as I've said."

"But I don't want a wife," Gareth whispered.

"What man does?"

Silence settled over the room like a fog. It choked them. The ticking clock on the mantle counted the seconds, drawing them out for an eternity.

Grandfather cleared his throat and stood. "This is Tabitha's chance at a happy life. Someone in this house should finally have one. It might as well be her."

Gareth looked up at his grandfather. "How would this marriage come about?"

Grandfather retrieved the empty glass and a crystal decanter from the fireplace. After returning to his seat at the desk, he popped the stopper and poured another glass. "You'd propose, just like any man. Marry her. Make her miserable, and send her home to America with her title."

"And the money?"

"Upon the announcement of your engagement to Miss Keller, her substantial dowry will be transferred to my account, and a new account opened for Tabitha's upkeep.

Your future wife is quite wealthy. She's filling our purse enough so that I can resume living in London, and you can live here." He took a sip from his refreshed glass.

Gareth's stomach was in knots. "So I marry her, and Tabitha gets the life she deserves. You get to live in the city as you prefer, and I get a wife I don't want. The only other option is for you and I to starve together as we send Tabitha off into the world alone?"

"Yes."

Gareth's stomach was in his throat, and he lost all appetite. The idea was impossible. He'd be forever in the chair. Forever keeping his secret from someone too close for comfort. It would be hell on earth. He wouldn't do it.

He balled his fist, ready to bring it down on the table beside him, but then he saw the painting of Tabitha on the wall. His sweet Tabitha, with those trusting eyes. There was no choice.

"I'll talk to Miss Keller's father tonight about courting her."

"There's no time for courting. Mr. Keller leaves Monday. You will propose tonight, and the wedding will be Saturday." He stood again, glass in hand.

Gareth choked. "So soon? What about the reading of the banns?"

"We will get a special license. They are not Anglican either. They attend some American church, so the wedding will be held here at Waverly Park."

Gareth glared at his grandfather. The desperation threatened to choke him. "I need more time."

Grandfather slammed a palm on the top of his wide desk, making the decanter jump on his blotter. "There isn't more time. You do this, or we send Tabitha off to a workhouse in the morning. Which will you have?"

The ticking clock resumed, but Gareth's heart seemed to have stopped. "I've no choice."

His grandfather produced a wide smile and came round his desk to pat him on the back. "I knew you'd do the right thing." He sat his half-empty glass on the table next to Gareth and walked out.

Gareth reached over, took his grandfather's glass, and turned it up. It burned his throat going down. That seemed right to him. It ought to burn when entering hell.

Chapter Six

They sat at the dinner table, all five of them. Gareth sat across from Mr. Keller and would rather have avoided him but found it necessary to make some sort of conversation with the man before asking for his daughter. Gareth cringed at the thought of matrimony. Sarah's herbed soup was usually his favorite, but with his stomach in knots, he could hardly swallow the broth.. Gareth forced it down before asking, "So you own some factories in America?"

Mr. Keller was a jolly looking man with dark hair and eyes like his daughter's. He was all smiles like her as well. Obviously not British. "Yes, textile factories. They turn cotton into thread and thread into fabrics. It used to take the families of everyone in town working day and night to fill our quota. But with our patented automations, one man does the work of five."

Gareth kept his expression to his normal look of boredom. "And the poor people put out of work? How do they feel about your success?"

Mr. Keller rubbed at his whiskers. "No one has been made jobless except the children, and we've endowed schools for them. Among the workers, we've re-educated the ones with a head for numbers and administrative work. We just built a park by the railroad tracks to greet newcomers, right across from the depot. The city of Chesnee, South Carolina, will be on the map soon as an example of what education and hard work can do."

"I see." The man was very unlike Grandfather. Most men of standing held no real occupation at all to speak of over a meal. If they did, they were only interested in growing their own purse, not helping those less fortunate. But Gareth couldn't show interest so he considered what his Grandfather might say. "And you are here, visiting your sister?"

That was good, like he wasn't interested in what was just said. "And how did she end up living here if she, too, is American?"

"In America, she married an Englishman. He grew homesick and moved back here, so I haven't seen her in years."

"And visiting her was what brought you here?"

Mr. Keller glanced over at Jessamine who appeared to blush. "That and other things."

Gareth glowered at her before looking back at his soup with disinterest. He didn't like her, but if she was in the room, he could never truly ignore her. If only she were harder to look at. If she had some ugly mole on her chin he could think about. Gareth glanced her way again, trying to find something disagreeable about her appearance, but his glance turned into a stare, and she caught him. He had to turn his attention back to his soup.

They finished dinner, and Grandfather invited the men to the library for drinks and cigars. Although Gareth followed, he chose not to indulge in either vice. It wasn't long before the room filled with men's chuckles and cigar smoke. Dizziness caused Gareth to waver and not pay close attention to what the older men discussed. A short while later, Grandfather excused himself and patted Gareth on the shoulder as he left. A cue.

Gareth angled his chair to view Jessamine's father. The gaslight surrounded the man in an orange glow. Gareth cleared his throat. "It has come to my attention that a match between your daughter and me would be advantageous for us all. Are you opposed to such a match?"

Mr. Keller sat, meeting him eye-to-eye. "I'm not opposed to it, if it's what she wants. She had her heart set on marrying an English gentleman and wouldn't consider any of the young men back in America. Honestly, she's the one to arrange this whole trip. I just want my little girl to be happy. It was my hope she'd find a love match like her mother and I have."

Gareth frowned at the man's last statement. "And you allow her such freedoms? Too much thinking and planning is said to be unhealthy for women. Do you care so little for her health?"

"Balderdash!" Mr. Keller's fist slammed down on the desk beside him. The normally jovial man's reaction took Gareth aback, but he concealed his shock. "Jessamine is just like her mother. They're both smart and know their own minds. They are both healthy as horses. That's fairy tale garbage spun by men with little minds. Jessamine's mother is just as much my business partner as my life partner. I'd hoped Jessamine would find such a match in life...I still do." The man looked Gareth in the eye on the last part. "If a stupid wife's what you want, you best not propose to my daughter."

Gareth shook his head. "I don't want any wife, stupid or smart, but I have no choice really."

Mr. Keller stood. "If you don't wish to marry my Jessamine, we'll be off. There are dozens of men back in America who do."

Gareth pushed his chair to block the man's passage. "But your daughter doesn't wish to marry them, as you, yourself, have stated. Besides, my grandfather's ward is anxious to join you and your wife in American society. So, let's cut to the chase. Do I have your permission to ask for Jessamine's hand?"

Mr. Keller studied Gareth, his cheeks red with anger. "You do. But I don't like it."

"Neither do I. Have the financial arrangements been worked out between you and my grandfather?"

Mr. Keller spoke through clenched teeth. "They have. My attorney has been in contact with his solicitor."

"Do you have a woman to accompany Tabitha with you back to America? I don't want her reputation tarnished in any way."

"She's two years my Jessie's junior and I'm a happily married, faithful husband. I'd never touch the girl. But, yes, my niece is also traveling with us. They will board together on the ship. No harm will come to your niece."

"My aunt," Gareth corrected and then let out a sigh. The first part of the blasted deed was done. "Then all that is left is for me to find Miss Keller and propose."

Gareth turned his chair to leave when the man stood and blocked his path. "Be good to her and try not to hurt her. Ever. That's all I ask."

Gareth gestured toward his legs. "I'm not a man capable of violence, as you can see. Your daughter is safe."

"There are many ways a man can hurt a woman. If one woman isn't enough for you, make sure my Jessie never finds out."

Gareth rolled his eyes. "Believe me, one woman is more than I want in my life. There won't be any others. Now please move before I change my mind and choose starvation."

Gareth wheeled himself out the door. Grandfather stood just outside, leaning against the banister.

"Is it done?" The old man fixed his eyes on Gareth, a look of expectation on his worried face.

"Yes. All that's left is for me to propose."

Grandfather nodded toward the evening room's door. "She's waiting for you on the terrace."

As Gareth started to push himself in that direction, his grandfather put his hand on his shoulder. "You've grown into a fine man, a far better man than I was at your age. Better than I am even now."

Gareth choked on the lump which formed in his throat and nodded at his grandfather. "I..." he swallowed. "I need to be done with this." And he wheeled himself down the way to the sitting room and onto the terrace where Jessamine stood.

Her crème colored dress with muted red flowers swayed in the breeze and hugged her figure. Gareth felt heat rush to his face. The cold night air filled his lungs. He drank it in.

She certainly wasn't difficult to look at. In fact, she grew prettier each time he saw her. Her cheeks were rosy in the cool air, and the breeze blew back the portion of hair pulled back but not up, as she looked at him expectantly. The longer he gazed at her, the harder it was to look away.

But it didn't matter how pretty she was; this would not be a love match. This slavery was forced on Gareth. It wrenched his gut to be coerced into anything. She was like the chair now, trapping him and labeling him. *Imprisoning him.* When he let his thoughts linger there rather than on her pretty face, it put a bad taste in his mouth, and he was ready to spew it all over her. This union wasn't even a *like* match.

"Miss Keller, how fortunate to find you alone out here. It's almost as if you were waiting for me."

Jessamine smiled. "Maybe I was."

"Yes, like a snake waiting in the rabbit's den." He narrowed his eyes at her.

Jessamine blinked hard and looked taken aback. "I am a snake and you are my prey? Is that how you see this?"

"How else am I to see it? Either throw Tabitha out to the wolves or sacrifice myself to you and give her a chance at a life."

This wasn't the topic he'd planned to speak on. He'd planned to get the proposal out of the way and over with, but his ire at the situation couldn't be contained.

Jessamine circled him, never backing down or looking offended. "Why so hostile? Why can't you see it as the offering a lifeline rather than a trap? I didn't create your grandfather's financial problems. My father and I have only offered a solution."

"Perhaps it is different in America, but here it is not polite to speak of finances."

"You were the one calling me a snake for trapping you. I was simply pointing out that I was offering a lifeline to you all."

"At the price of me and my future title."

Jessamine turned and placed her hands on her hips. "Well, maybe it's not your title that interests me about you. Maybe I couldn't care less about such things. Maybe what I want from you… " Jessamine stepped toward him and bent down until her face was inches from his, "is far more interesting than a title."

Gareth swallowed. Jessamine's floral fragrance mixed with what had to be her natural essence, and it clouded his mind. He held his breath in order to think. Her eyes were as teasing as her scent was maddening. The way she leaned over him caused her modest décolletage to become less modest. He forced his eyes shut in order to think.

Why was he angry with her? Right, she was forcing him to live life in the blasted chair. Forcing him to hide in his own home. The anger returned. Anger—his go-to emotion.

"Step. Back. Miss Keller." Gareth's tone was harsh and commanding.

When he sensed she no longer stood close, he opened his eyes. Jessamine had retreated against the balcony railing. A calculating smile played on her lips. She always looked like she had him figured out already.

"Oh, let's get this over with, shall we?"

Jessamine motioned for him to proceed.

"Miss Keller, will you honor me by agreeing to become my wife?"

Jessamine's brows furrowed as her hands went to her hips. "Is that it? That's how you're going to propose to me?"

Gareth grimaced at the girl. "Well, I can't get on one knee, obviously."

She shook her head. "I didn't mean that."

She seemed frustrated by his comment but not embarrassed the way most people were when he mentioned his disability.

"Then what do you want?"

"I don't know. Presenting me with a family ring? Maybe some romantic words?"

Gareth repositioned his chair to better his view of her. "Grandfather sold all the rings, and I thought of starting with how much I ardently admire and love you, but I choked on the vomit that came up when I tried to say it."

Jessamine stared in silence at first only to burst into laughter a second later. "Now that was perfect. I love honesty above all else. Yes, I will marry you. I think this will be fun for both of us."

How insane. He observed her thoughtfully. "You must have a different idea of fun in America."

She moved closer, extended her hand, and ran her fingers through his hair. A shiver shot down his spine. It took all his effort to keep the reaction from showing. He remained still as stone.

"Don't think I don't see who is really beneath the armor."

Gareth held a breath, stiffening at her words.

"You put up this steel armor around yourself in the form of hostility and disinterest—whichever works to shield you best at the moment, but that's not who you are." Her voice was no longer girlish but husky and seductive. Just the sound affected him, and his skin prickled.

Gareth coughed, clearing his throat and mind so he could speak. "And who am I?"

She bent lower. Gareth swallowed, bracing himself for the onslaught on his senses.

Her breath brushed against his skin as she whispered, "You are a man who cares so much it scares you. You not only care, you act on it. You could let Tabitha's fate be as uncertain as your own, but you love her. You see someone in trouble, and you act. You'd probably do this same thing for your grandfather. You put the welfare of others before yours."

She leaned back, and Gareth suddenly felt cold in the absence of her breath on his neck. Her voice returned to conversational tone. "I hope you let me see beneath the armor someday. I look forward to earning your affection and your trust."

Gareth let out his breath in relief. "You credit me with too much. You know nothing of me. My anger's no armor. It's just anger. And my disinterest in you is genuine." He looked away, no longer able to take her seductive gaze.

"I know you are a man with secrets. And I plan to know them all."

Gareth whipped his head in her direction and gripped the arms of his chair. "My secrets are mine. You can force my hand into this marriage, but you cannot force my hand beyond the portion of my life I plan to share with you. As of now, I plan to share no more than my name and title. Marriage does not give you any rights beyond that."

Jessamine crossed her arms over her chest. "Don't worry. I don't plan to pry them from you. I'll wait for you to offer them of your own free will."

"And when will I do that?"

"The day you fall in love with me."

Gareth turned his chair and began rolling away. The moment he entered the sitting room, Sarah stepped in and announced, "Coffee and dessert are served."

Gareth shook his head and didn't slow his progress as he pushed past her. "I've lost my appetite. Give Grandfather my apologies. I'm going back to my room."

Chapter Seven

Once the house was quiet and all had settled in for the night, Gareth shot up from his bed and flew to his trunk where he kept his armor. He'd made adjustments to it through the years to make it more comfortable. He'd widened the joints for his growing form.

The silver helmet shone in the gaslight. He pulled it on and lowered the visor. He was about to grab his usual sword, the short sword he'd found years ago in the attic. But his eyes fell on the claymore that lay against the wall at the footboard of his bed. *A mystery.* Who had sent it and why? It was much larger and heavier than the one he practiced with at

Mr. Strong's. Gareth swung it about, eager to give it a try. The size and weight of the claymore felt awkward.

He pushed open the doors to the balcony and set out over the trees with sword overhead, swinging it in pretend fight. No one had ever challenged the Flying Knight. Most just ran away in fear. He wondered if he could actually use the sword if the need arose. Because Mr. Strong rarely held back in their swordplay, Gareth felt confident in his skills. The old man treated him as any other student, and it had made the tutor one of Gareth's favorite people. He still visited the old man for that reason.

The cool night air seeped into the joints of his armor and wicked away the sweat that had formed during his practice. He was in mid-swing of his make-believe sword fight in the sky when he caught sight of a figure on the road below. He sheathed his sword and descended to the trees for cover. Who was on the road so late? The form was female, and her dress clung to her in an oddly familiar way. As he drew closer, Gareth recognized the crème and rose dress from earlier.

He scowled. What was she doing out here?

Jessamine hurried along the road toward town. Her brown hair had been partially swept up into a coiffeur earlier, but it now hung loose around her face. He descended to stand in her path, akimbo. His armor caused an echo, making his voice sound distant and unfamiliar. "Halt!"

The full moon cast pale light on her dark eyes and the pink in her cheeks. A grin spread across her face. "It's you."

Gareth was at a loss for words. What was he doing? He normally only disturbed what looked like a crime in progress. "Miss, it is not safe for a lady to be out walking alone. I advise you to hurry back to where you came and wait until the morning for whatever errand you are on. Nothing is open in the town this late."

"I'm on my way to visit my cousin so I might share my good news. I'm to be married."

Just like a silly girl to be out alone for such a foolish reason. "I must insist you wait to go in the morning. It's not safe now."

"Actually, I've heard the town is quite safe, all because of you. I was hoping to meet you." She stepped closer. "And now I have."

The way she gazed at him in the moonlight mesmerized him. Gareth couldn't think as the breeze stirred her hair and blew her floral aroma in his direction. It was then something whistled past his ear, brushing against his helmet. It made a thud sound behind him. He jerked his head in that direction. An arrow stuck out of the tree trunk. The faint sound of another whistle put him on high alert. Time seemed to slow as adrenaline coursed through his veins. Another arrow headed for Jessamine. Gareth grabbed her in his arms and turned. The arrow glanced off the back of his armor with a metallic ring.

Jessamine screamed when the next arrow just missed them. Shielding her with his body, he took flight, cradling her against him.

In his chest, his heart raced harder, helping him fly faster than he ever had. He spun in the air like a log rolling in a river, avoiding the arrows as they followed. He climbed higher and headed for the cover of the forest. Once in the top of the tall pines, he settled Jessamine on a limb.

"Stay here. I've got to go check and see who was shooting those."

Her eyes were large with fright. "Was that a normal occurrence for you?"

"No!" Gareth looked back toward the direction of the town. "It seems not everyone is happy to have a flying knight patrolling the shire. I'll be back. I promise."

Jessamine grabbed his arm with both hands and met his eyes through the visor. Hers were desperate, huge, and full of concern. Gareth reached out and cupped her face with his gloved hand. "Don't be afraid. I won't leave you here for long."

She nodded and gripped the tree. "Go, before he gets away."

"Right."

Gareth took flight. He held his arms close to his sides to increase speed. He reached the path where the arrows had rained down and followed where they might have come. He made his way to a copse several yards away. He found a patch of tall grass lying flat and a few stray arrows. A small pool of red glistened in the moonlight. Gareth set his jaw. Blood. He took off and skimmed over the trees and below the canopy searching for any stir. He found another drop of blood a few yards away but no more flattened grass.

Scooping up the arrows, he stashed them in the sheath with his sword and headed back to the pines. He found Jessamine standing in the tree, peering down with a smile.

Gareth flew up to her. "Are you not afraid of heights?"

She smiled wider and shook her head. "No, I love being up high, looking down on the world. Arrows flying at me—that I'm afraid of. Did you see anyone?"

Gareth shook his head. "No."

"Has this happened before? Are you always in danger when you go out?"

"No. Never. Until tonight." He mumbled to himself, "You really are bad luck."

"What?"

"Nothing. Whoever it was, he's gone now. I'd best get you back home before I do any more investigating."

Gareth took hold of Jessamine and flew toward his estate.

Jessamine's arms encircled Gareth's neck, her face only inches from his. Even in the armor, he could feel how warm and soft her body was. He sometimes flew with Tabitha, but this was different. Tabitha was like a sister, but Jessamine's scent affected him.

"You smell like flowers."

"It's yellow jessamine, the flower I'm named for. My mother had it made for me as a birthday gift."

"No wonder it suits you."

Gareth descended to the balcony of Jessamine's guest room, and set her on her feet. He stood at attention.

"How did you know where I was staying?"

Gareth realized his blunder. He coughed. "I…know…all."

"Now I'd believe that if I thought you a phantom."

She stepped toward him, and Gareth took to flight. "I have to track the path of the archer. Please take my advice and stay in at night from now on."

"But then how will I see you again?"

"You won't."

Gareth hurled himself through the air, back toward the spot he'd found the arrows. Jessamine was a distraction indeed. How would he handle himself around her once she was his wife? How would he keep her at a distance so as to continue his work as the Flying Knight? And who was out tonight trying to shoot him with arrows?

He didn't know the answers to any of his questions, but he'd have to find a solution to all of them, fast. His protective metal gear would take care of the issue of an archer out to get him for now. But the solution of what to do about Jessamine would take more than a suit of armor.

Gareth arrived back at the patch of flattened grass and blood. He flew around it, trying to find a track to follow.

Only there wasn't one. Just the second drop of blood. No trail in any direction. It was almost as if the archer had also taken flight.

His breath caught as he glanced about. Was there someone else with the ability to fly? At that thought, Gareth moved his investigation higher. He found more blood on the limb of a tree near the flatten patch. It was times like this Gareth wished he knew more about his ability and its origins. Did flying run in the family? And how would he ask his grandfather such a question? If it was from his mother's side, he didn't even know anyone to ask.

He knew nothing of his mother. Only that she was from Scotland and had left him. Was she still alive? Did he even care if she was?

Gareth headed into town and flew about. Most of the houses had already grown dark for the night, but he found a light on at Mr. Strong's house. He flew down to try to investigate but the heavy beige curtains were drawn tight. Although they sifted the light through, he couldn't even see any shapes on the other side.

He started to knock on the door but then realized he was in armor. If he took it off and hid it, Mr. Strong would ask about his chair.

Gareth lit upon a high branch in his favorite oak tree in town and watched Mr. Strong's house for an hour. Finally, the light went out. Nothing suspicious. The old man was probably reading or having a cup of tea.

Early morning light began to highlight the eastern horizon. Gareth yawned and headed back to his room. He slowly opened his balcony door and looked around. Never again would he fly in without checking first. Gareth changed out of the armor and into his nightclothes. He hid his armor in the trunk.

After climbing into his bed, he reached over to douse the light when he caught sight of one of the arrows in his sword's scabbard. He withdrew from his bed and snatched one. He examined the arrowhead, twisting and turning it in the gaslight. Someone had tried to kill him. They had almost killed Jessamine. And though he couldn't be certain, it seemed likely that person could fly. What had changed in his life that would suddenly bring this threat? There was the claymore that had arrived from nowhere. He'd have to question Sarah and Thompton further to find out who had delivered it. Did they sign for it? What company had shipped it?

Knowing the assailant could fly meant it wasn't some hoodlum from the shire trying to rid the town of its protector. This was someone who knew something about Gareth, maybe more about him than he knew himself.

A knock sounded at his chamber door.

"Who is it?" He tucked the arrow quickly under his mattress, turned off his lamp, and laid his head on his soft feather pillow.

His door opened slightly. He expected to see Sarah or Tabitha, but instead it was Jessamine, carrying a lamp with her. "I thought I saw a light and heard stirring in here." She padded in softly. "I just feel terrible about earlier. I didn't mean to make you so angry with my proposition. I don't want to start this marriage with you already feeling resentment toward me."

Jessamine's floral fragrance still lingered on him, and when she walked in, the stronger scent mingled. He cleared his throat. "It's late and would not be appropriate for you to be found in my room alone. You should go."

The golden light glowed on her face, and her dark hair shone like a raven's feathers. "Yes, you're right." She turned and left, closing the door behind her.

Gareth let out a breath he didn't know he'd been holding. He shook his head and rolled over to try to get at least a little sleep. His mind wandered back to the soft body he'd held in his arms a few hours earlier. Soon she would be his wife. That thought lead to all kinds of possibilities he'd never allowed himself to entertain before. He wasn't sure he should even entertain them now. What if he couldn't control his ability to fly, and right in the middle of consummating the marriage, he realized they were on the ceiling. He clenched his fists. No, the marriage would be in name only.

And what of this attempted assassination? Did the assailant know Gareth was the Flying Knight somehow? Would he attack the house? Soon Grandfather and Tabitha would be gone, but Jessamine would still be there. He couldn't put her at risk, either.

He closed his eyes at the thought. How could he investigate all this without her finding out his secret? And how would he keep her safe from whoever was trying to kill him?

The best thing to do would be to continue to push her away until she shipped herself back to America with her title as his estranged wife. The sooner that happened, the better.

Gareth finally drifted off to a fitful sleep, full of dreams of hidden archers and Jessamine in his arms, heading for the ceiling.

Chapter Eight

Gareth sat at his wing chair. He had asked to take his breakfast in his room. After his restless four hours of sleep, he had no interest in seeing the Kellers or Grandfather. And there was still the archer at large. It might be safer for everyone if the assassin didn't find them in the same room with him, *if* the assassin knew he was the Flying Knight.

Sarah brought up Gareth's tray and placed it on his desk next to the wing chair.

"Mornin' sir. Ye look a bit frazzled fer so early. Ye na be hurt or feelin' unwell I hope." She eyed Gareth up and down as if seeking out an ailment.

"No, I'm fine. Just tired."

"Happy to hear it." She nodded and opened the tray and butter dish before pouring tea. She winced and supported her arm with the other. A bandage wrapped around her forearm.

"What's wrong with your arm?"

Sarah glanced down at the bandage. A strange look came over her before she answered. "Oh, clumsy me. I burnt it whilst cookin' this mornin'. I put some butter on it before wrappin' it up."

Sarah turned to leave, but Gareth stopped her. "Sarah, you and Thompton are from Scotland. So was my mother."

The ginger-haired woman turned with a grin. "Really? Lord Pensees didna mention that."

"Not surprising. My father came home from a holiday with a wife who had no family connections. It wasn't Grandfather's proudest moment."

Sarah nodded. "Oh."

"But I don't know anything about Scotland or my mother's family."

Sarah clapped her hands. "Scotland is beautiful. Especially the highlands where I'm from. The woods there be deep and full of magical creatures."

"What kinds of creatures?"

"Oh, fairies. They live beyond the wooded curtain which can only be opened to one of their clan."

Gareth scrunched his forehead. "Fairies? You mean the tiny people with wings?"

Sarah shook her head. "Na, yer thinkin' of pixies. They be distant cousins of the Fae folk. Fairies be the size of humans, but they do'na fly with wings. They fly by fairy magic. It hits on the eve of adulthood."

Gareth narrowed his eyes. "Like around twelve years?"

Sarah nodded. "Aye, 'bout then. God wouldna be so daft as to stick a mother with the responsibility of a flying baby."

"And the magic, can it do anything besides make them fly?"

"Different Fae folk have different gifts. Some can only fly. Some are changelings and can take the form of other people or animals at will. Some are healers. But those are always women of noble birth. And there be the Seelie and Unseelie courts." Sarah's face took on a distant, despondent look.

"What's the difference?"

Sarah started busying herself with putting Gareth's bed to right as she spoke. "The Seelie be a loving clan. They find nourishment in love and family. They sicken among the land of men, where selfishness and hate rule. They stick to the deep wood, far from all that. The Unseelie tend to na be so organized. They feed off anger and resentment. They make a home among the worst of humans where they grow strong. But because of their very nature of animosity and discord, they be na able to gain strength as a court."

Gareth's brow furrowed as he listened. "Are the two courts enemies?"

Sarah nodded. "Aye, but the problem comes when a Seelie becomes Unseelie. All that need happen is to allow bitterness to take root. Unseelies almost never become Seelies, because once the bitterness takes root, it corrupts the soul. It's na impossible to go back, but 'tis a very hard road."

Gareth was about to ask another question when a knock sounded on his chamber door. Grandfather stepped in.

"Sarah, do you know where I can find Thompton? I need a carriage ready but he's not in the stable."

A forlorn look swept over her face. "Nay, sir. I'm sorry. I have na seen him this mornin'. I'll go see if I can find him."

"Please do. His job might not pay well, but he won't have it much longer if I can't count on him to be where he's supposed to be."

Sarah bowed her head. "Yes, m'lord."

Her hands trembled by her sides as Grandfather stormed out. She started for the door without looking when Tabitha burst through with her mutt in her arms.

"Sarah, I'm so glad I found you." Tabitha blew her still loose blonde hair from her face. "I just found Rory in the attic. He's bleeding."

Sarah met Tabitha's gaze, her eyes full of genuine concern. She took the dog from her and held him close. Her eyes closed as she whispered, "Thank ye, Jesus." She cradled the animal to her as she addressed Tabitha. "Ye go on and finish getting' dressed while I treat his wounds with some a me herbs. Can ye manage without me while I take care of the dog?"

Tabitha's blue eyes were still moist. "I can dress myself. Do you think he'll be ok?" She nodded toward her dog, Rory.

Sarah smiled. "Aye. He'll be just fine once he be treated with me herbs. That and a bit a rest. He will be up and 'bout in na time."

Sarah walked out the door, dog in arms. Gareth heard her whispering what sounded like, "I love ye so much. Ye had me comin' out me skin with worry."

Gareth started on his eggs when he noticed Tabitha watching him. He set down his fork. "What?"

Tabitha grinned. "Congratulations."

Gareth rolled his eyes. "Oh that. Congratulations to you and your future as an American."

"I think Jessamine is perfect for you. You have a very good chance at happiness with her."

He waved his hands toward her in a shooing gesture. "Would you go and let me eat in peace? Talking about my intended is making me lose my appetite."

Tabitha shook her head as she made her way out, closing the door behind her.

***

Gareth wheeled himself up the ramp to Mr. Strong's door and knocked. There wasn't any answer, so he knocked again. Still no answer. Gareth was about to turn his chair around and leave when he noticed a smudge on the door frame. A red-brown thumbprint. *Blood.*

Memories of the night before flashed before his eyes. The blood in the forest. Mr. Strong's house lit up in the middle of the night. Gareth's eyes darted, and he made sure no one was watching. Then he flew from his chair and backed away from the door, just before flying at it with his shoulder. He bumped into the door and fell back against his chair. He shot up, away, and did it again. This time the door gave.

Gareth flew in and stopped. Right in the middle of the floor was a pool of blood. Gareth glanced around and noticed the desk, chair, and cupboard were all overturned. Papers and swords littered the floor.

Gareth flew to the kitchen. "Mr. Strong?" he called as loud as he could. The kitchen chairs had been turned over and much of the countertop items scattered. He flew for the bedroom and pushed the door open. The mattress lay bare. Not even a sheet or blanket.

Gareth hovered around the house. His many thoughts rushed through his mind in a jumble. Where was Mr. Strong? Was that his blood? Was Mr. Strong involved in the attempt on his life? He shook his head at the idea. The man had plenty of chances to kill him during swordplay.

But he was quite skilled in swords. Perhaps he knew archery, as well. Or was Mr. Strong a victim, caught up in the middle of this? Maybe he had tangled with whoever had tried to kill Gareth last night? Had the old man been tortured and murdered for knowing him?

Panic rose, and his heart raced. Gareth flew out to the porch and shut the door before getting in his chair and heading back to the manor, posthaste.

There would be a wedding in a few days. If he could just make sure Tabitha and Grandfather stayed safe until then, they would leave and be away from whatever was going on. Then there would only be Jessamine, Sarah, and Thompton. Sarah and Thompton would be easy. He'd fire them. With no servants and a grouch for a husband, surely Jessamine would be back to America in a hurry.

He pushed the wheels harder. The rocks and loose dirt crunched as he rolled over them.

But there was still the question of why someone tried to kill Gareth and why the assassin seemed to have the ability to fly. Why could Gareth fly? He knew the answer was connected to his mother and Scotland somehow. He'd have to arrange a trip there to find out more about the Fae and where his mother came from.

Gareth wheeled into the house through the back kitchen entrance. Rory was on a pallet resting. The side where he'd been bleeding earlier sported an herbal poultice.

Gareth reached down and petted the mutt. "Looks like you had a rough night, too."

The dog whined.

"I'm sorry you were hurt. Did the archer attack you? Is no one I keep company with safe? Not even the dog?"

Gareth's gut wrenched at the thought of whatever had become of Mr. Strong. Was there any chance the man still lived? Gareth had to hope. He couldn't bear the thought of the man dead. But what of the amount of blood at his house?

Nausea rolled over Gareth at the pictures in his imagination. What had become of Mr. Strong?

Bile rose again. Gareth clamped his hand over his mouth and made his way back to the door. He was sick in a patch of grass. It wasn't just the remembrance of the pooled blood but the stress of it all. He needed to figure all this out. On his own. There was no one he could share this with. Jessamine was the only other person who knew about the archer, but she wasn't someone he could confide in. How would Grandfather react if he was told? Tabitha was leaving for a happy life in America. Why bring her down into it?

Gareth wiped his mouth and made his way back to the house. Rory stared at him, a look of sympathy in the dog's eyes.

"I'm all right boy. You just rest and heal. No need burdening you with my problems either."

Gareth made his way to the stairs where he listened for any stirring. Only the ticking of the grandfather clock broke the silence. He took the chance and flew up the stairs to his room. Once inside, he made his way to his trunk and pulled out the claymore. He slashed it overhead, spinning and turning as he went. He took his practice to the air. It still felt heavy in his hands. If he was at war, he needed to be battle ready for his next flight out.

Chapter Nine

Gareth stood in front of the mirror in his chamber, preparing for dinner. He had sent word that he would take dinner in his room, but Grandfather had quickly denied his request. Grandfather ordered Gareth to join the party for dinner and expected him to help entertain their guests. Gareth struggled with his cravat as he glared at it in the mirror. An expletive escaped under his breath as he tried to tie it again. He had more important things on his mind, like how to protect everyone associated with him. Entertaining the annoying Americans only added to his stress

Where was Mr. Strong? Was he already dead? The old man was never far from Gareth's thoughts. It gnawed at his gut, keeping him on the edge of retching his stomach's contents again. Was the old man being tortured for information at that very moment—information he didn't have? Guilt at what might be happening to Mr. Strong twisted his insides further into a knot. *The old man was probably already dead.*

Regardless of his grandfather's demands, Gareth contemplated refusing to join the dinner party. He had no appetite and didn't think he'd find it by dinner.

Who was the flying attacker and from where had he come? Should he attack again, how would Gareth guard everyone at Waverly Park? The weight of being the household's sole protector pushed down on him. It felt so heavy he could barely stand with it on his shoulders. If only he could confide in Tabitha, but she was heading to her new life very soon so he might as well get used to being utterly alone.

Argh. He ripped the stupid, frivolous fabric from around his neck. Tabitha usually tied them for him. Another reminder of all that he faced.

A gentle knock sounded at the door.

Gareth wadded the cravat into a crumpled mess and threw it across the room. "To hell with you!"

The door opened. "'Come in,' is what we say in America. You'll have to help me with English etiquette when we entertain guests, or I'll get it all wrong for sure." The melodic voice swept into the room uninvited, just like its owner. Jessamine shut the door behind her and blinked at Gareth. "You're standing?"

"Here it is customary to wait until granted entrance before barging into a room. I might have been indecent." Gareth continued facing forward, choosing to glare at her from his reflection while keeping his back to her. "And yes, I can stand. I simply cannot walk."

Jessamine padded across the floor in slippered feet, heading for Gareth. "I just wanted to have a talk with you before dinner. There's something I think I should tell you." Jessamine's dark eyes widened as she noticed the cravat on the floor. Her pink dress rustled as she bent to retrieve it. He'd seen her décolletage was a bit lower, as was customary for evening dresses and still respectable. But now, the combined effect of her corset and her bending allowed Gareth to steal a view of her womanly endowments. He had to glance away so he could think and remember why he didn't want her around.

"Miss Keller, it really isn't proper for you to be in my chamber with the door closed. I suggest that whatever you need to say can wait until we are at dinner or in one of the common rooms with an open door."

Jessamine continued on her path to Gareth, stepping between him and the mirror. Her floral scent replaced the air as he breathed. His mind felt as if he'd had too much to drink when she stood so close. The warmth of her body radiated from her, and the memory of holding her rushed in, making his hands want to reach for her. Gareth cleared his throat. "Miss Keller, please leave before your father discovers you here."

Jessamine reached up and placed the cravat around Gareth's neck, bringing her face just inches from his as she stretched up on her toes. Her large, dark eyes teased him, and she smiled. "And what will he do if he finds us here? Force a hasty marriage upon us?"

Gareth returned a stern look at her comment.

Jessamine giggled as she arranged Gareth's cravat and straightened his collar. "I'm sorry, but what I need to tell you is of the utmost importance and isn't for other ears. I know you aren't pleased with this match between us. I'm hoping that in time you might soften toward me. But it will never happen if we keep secrets from each other." Her eyes no longer teased as she looked up at Gareth. "Last night I went out for a walk after everyone was in bed. My reasons were twofold. I wanted to share the good news of our engagement with my cousin—"

"Good news indeed," Gareth interrupted.

Jessamine pursed her lips but continued. "Anyway, my second purpose...I was hoping to get a glimpse of the Flying Knight. I failed at the first reason, but...I did more than succeed in the other."

Gareth hadn't expected this confession and wasn't sure how to respond. He forced what he hoped looked like an expression of disbelief. "You saw the Flying Knight? Are you certain it wasn't a bat?" He raised one eyebrow in mocking disbelief for effect.

Jessamine's hands went to her hips. "You don't believe me?" Her lips parted in a look of astonishment.

"I think it's preposterous. How could you have seen this phantom during your short visit to the shire, when neither I nor anyone else in our household has ever seen him? He's always spotted by the overly imaginative or simpletons." Gareth shook his head. "On second thought, it makes perfect sense that you spotted him."

Jessamine narrowed her eyes and shot him a look of pure death. "I'm neither simple nor did I imagine the whole thing. And he had to be one big bat because I did more than see him. I flew with him."

Gareth stared blankly at her. "You went flying with him?" Gareth pointed at the ceiling. "Up in the air? How much celebrating did you and Tabitha do once you excused yourselves?"

Her dark eyes flared. "I wasn't drunk. He flew me to safety because someone shot arrows at us… well, at him, but I was there, so he swooped me up and took me to safety before going to investigate." She stepped closer to Gareth, taking his hands and wrapping them around her waist before putting her arms around his neck. "I was this close to him—so close I could feel the warmth of his body through the armor. He's no phantom. He's living flesh. I could hear his pounding heart." Her dark eyes met his. "Much like I can hear yours now."

Gareth swallowed. "And you're telling me this dream you had last night because...? Is this some attempt to make me jealous?"

Jessamine stepped back. "It was no dream. And no, I'm not attempting to make you jealous. You'll soon be my husband and protector. These are your lands and your village. The knight said he'd never been attacked like that before so this could be some new danger for your household and neighboring people. I thought you needed to know."

Gareth's glare became even more acrid. "Protector? Have you been blind to the wheelchair I sit in, day-in and day-out? I'm in no position to be anyone's protector. If that's what you want, maybe you should flag down your flying knight and marry him instead."

Jessamine shook her head. "I came to you with this as a way to start building trust between us. You are not just some cripple stuck in a chair with nothing to offer. You're a man with strengths and abilities. Honestly, I believe you think of your chair as an impediment much more than anyone else does." Jessamine spun around. "Look, it's not even in the room, and you have to bring it up." She stopped and a curious expression came over her lovely face. "How do you get around in here without your chair? How did you get to the mirror where you stand?"

Gareth held her gaze while trying to think of an answer. Then he remembered that he needed to drive her away. He knew just how. "Like this." Gareth hopped and hobbled toward the nearby chair. Before he got there he intentionally stumbled to the floor.

Jessamine started toward him.

"Don't. I can do this." Gareth crawled his way up the chair and sat. "This is how your future protector gets about without his chair. Do you think this attacker will fear me when he sees me crawling toward him? Or maybe he'll worry I can run him down with my chair?" Gareth was yelling at that point. His face grew hot from his rage at having to move about in such an undignified manner in front of her. "Does this arouse you? Look at me, the man you will soon marry. Get a good look because this is what you will be chained to for the rest of your life. You want honesty? This is what I am without my chair. If you must have your title so much, then take it and get on the ship with it, along with Tabitha and your father. Let's not pretend this marriage is about any more than your rung on the social ladder."

Tears pooled in Jessamine's eyes, and her lip quivered. "I didn't mean to upset you or...cause you embarrassment." She stepped toward him, reaching out her hand. "I'm really not..."

"You're not what? Interested in marrying me? Good. Go without the title. Even better. That way we have no ties at all. I'll do this for Tabitha if I must, but don't expect me to pretend to be happy about any of it. If it wasn't for her needing a secure future I'd not suffer your presence a moment longer. Now get out of my room!"

127

Jessamine blinked hard and stumbled toward the door. She turned to face Gareth one last time when she got there. "I was going to say that I'm really not bothered by how you move without your chair. I want to be your partner in life and help you. I hope someday you feel comfortable being your true self in front of me."

"This *is* my true self."

Jessamine nodded and walked out the door.

The hurt look on Jessamine's face weighed on Gareth. She annoyed him, yes, but inflicting her pain bothered him. But he had no choice. It was for her safety anyway. How could he ever respect or trust a woman who only wanted him for a title? She'd have her title soon enough and be back on a boat for America.

Besides, Gareth would need to do some traveling himself. He needed to go to Scotland and find out more about his mother and the Fae. Had she been one of them? Perhaps Grandfather had more information he could draw from.

Chapter Ten

The next morning, Gareth flew back and forth in his chamber listening to the chaos in the house. Strange voices calling back and forth to one another. The grunts of men hefting furniture and scrapes as they moved it and then the thud of it being set back down.

Gareth punched the ceiling before descending to the bedroom door and peeking out again. He was dying to get out of the confines of his four chamber walls, while at the same time trying to stay out of the way of all the workers preparing the house for the blasted wedding.

He zoomed to the curtains and glanced down at the yard. Carts, loaded with flowers and food, were arriving.

There were even some of the new automobiles parked in front of Waverly Park.

The now familiar sound of feminine laughter down the hall grated at Gareth's last nerve. Jessamine would become his wife that very night. He surveyed the yard once more. It didn't matter who was in the house, he had to get out at least for the day.

Gareth flew to the door and peeked out. Unfamiliar women in maid uniforms carried linens down the hall. He closed the door again and banged his head on it. He needed to call the whole thing off. He couldn't go through with it. The idea of cold feet became reality for him.

His heart raced, and sweat ran from his forehead to his chin. He could just leave. Fly away. Maybe go to Scotland and never come back. Down the hall, Tabitha laughed. The melodic ring of her voice put steel in his spine. There was no money and no choice. For Tabitha's sake, there was no escaping the ordeal to come.

He could do this. He just needed to get outside and get away for a bit. After waiting until no one was looking, he made his way down the stairs, into his chair, and out the back door. He glanced up at his majestic ancestral home. Waverly Park was a large stone estate, built twelve generations back. The inside had always been as cold and gray as the stone on the outside when Tabitha was absent. She was the only one to ever touch his heart. He'd do all in his power to establish her future. She'd even softened Grandfather's stone heart through the years. He had to keep them safe. It was his duty.

After his encounter with Jessamine, he defied Grandfather after all and skipped dinner. Once everyone was in bed, he had patrolled into the early morning, looking for any signs of the archer, but the attacker had not returned. Perhaps he was lying low, waiting for a more opportune moment to attack. Gareth only hoped that would be after Tabitha and all the guests were gone.

Gareth was passing the stable when he noticed Thompton setting down a crate and stopping to eye him. The man nodded when he saw Gareth looking, and Gareth returned the gesture. He had never interacted with the ruddy-looking man much. Thompton mostly stayed in the stables, and when he was in the house, Sarah did all the talking for him.

He wondered how old Thompton and Sarah were. They'd been a fixture at Waverly Park as far back as he could remember and yet still looked to be in their prime. Both were strong, hard working, and loyal. Gareth thought about the couple's impending dismissal and felt it gnaw at his gut. When Grandfather had to cut everyone's pay and all the other servants left, they'd stayed. He'd have to give them some kind of severance package for such loyalty, to help them until they found work. That and a letter of recommendation and they should be fine.

He pushed on toward Mr. Strong's house, remembering the disarray there. Sarah and Thompton must leave, before they were hurt by whoever had attacked Gareth and harmed Mr. Strong. He couldn't have another victim on his conscience whose only crime was being associated with him.

Gareth pushed himself up the ramp and sat in front of Mr. Strong's door. He eyed a young woman walking along the road with a toddler. She nodded a greeting, and he nodded back. Gareth knocked on the door in pretense. His plan was to force the door open once they'd passed so he could further investigate. But he was not able to follow through since the door opened.

Gareth stared up from his chair into the face of Mr. Strong. Gareth's breath caught.

"Gareth, so nice of you to come. I wasn't expecting to see you until tonight."

Gareth's mouth hung open as his eyes refused to so much as blink.

The old man, very much alive and unharmed, stared back at him. "Are you all right? You look as if you've seen a ghost."

Gareth shook it off. "I...um... came by yesterday, but no one answered. I was worried."

The old man stepped aside and motioned for Gareth to enter. "No need to worry. I went home to visit my wife." The old man grinned and punched Gareth in the shoulder. "Soon you'll know all about the pleasures of matrimony."

Gareth pushed his chair cautiously into the house, taking the room in. The cupboard was back in its place as was everything else. But on the floor where the pooled blood had been was a rug. "The rug is new."

The old man smiled. "Yes, the wife sent it with me. She worries that the place looks too sparse."

Gareth swallowed. "Right."

He must have looked as distracted as he felt when he answered the old man. Mr. Strong stepped into his line of sight while he surveyed the rest of the room. "You seem out of sorts. Is it the wedding? Are you nervous?"

Gareth plastered on a stiff smile. "Aren't most men nervous about their life coming to an end?"

Mr. Strong's eyes warmed. "Marriage isn't quite that. I suppose getting nervous about the commitment is normal, but I never was. I knew I was making the best decision of my life. You might find wedded bliss suits you." Again the man punched Gareth in the arm. "And the benefits might leave you smiling enough to wipe that constant scowl away for good." The man chuckled.

Gareth's mind raced, trying to force some kind of logical explanation for what he saw and was now seeing. He was hardly listening to the man when it finally registered what the old man was implying. Heat rose into Gareth's face.

The old man pulled up a chair to sit and look Gareth in the eye. "Do you have any questions or concerns about…tonight? You haven't been like the other dandy men, chasing the skirts of easy women."

Gareth's temper flared. Who was this man to talk to him like that? He'd considered the man his friend and mentor, but he was obviously hiding something. *The liar.* What else about him was false? Was there even a wife?

"You don't know what I've done or who I've been with. I don't tell you everything." Gareth spat the words at the man and backed his chair away from him.

The old man stood. "All right, all right. Didn't mean to embarrass ye none. Just wanted to let ye know if you have any questions, I'd be willing to answer 'em."

Gareth stared at him. The accent change brought back memories of the swordplay, and the times the man had charged at him with a sword, forcing Gareth to use his flight or die. Had the man noticed or known all along? Or was Mr. Strong trying to kill him all those times? Gareth spun around in his chair. "I'm sure I've got it under control. I should get back."

Mr. Strong opened the door but stepped in front of him and blocked the entrance. "But you just got here."

"I just remembered some things I need to settle before this evening."

The old man grinned. "I'll see you this evening at the wedding. Say, why did you come by if it wasn't for some advice about tonight?"

Gareth shook his head. "No reason." He glanced at the rug and then back up at the old man before making his way down the ramp.

Mr. Strong knew something about it all. Was the old man in on the attack? What was he hiding?

The next question came to mind—whose blood was pooled on Mr. Strong's floor if it had not been that of Mr. Strong?

Gareth's mind was a mess. He wheeled into his drive. The place was even more crowded with people.

"Bloody hell!"

Gareth wheeled to the back and entered through the kitchen, but that too was packed worse than a can of sardines. At least by that evening, the whole event would be over. But now what was he to do? Mr. Strong wasn't in danger. Did that mean the rest of the household was safe? Or was Mr. Strong the source of danger?

He hid in a corner, waiting for a chance to fly to his room, but there was none. People dashed in and out of the foyer constantly.

"Do ye need help up the stairs, sir?"

Gareth looked up to see Thompton. "No, I'm quite all right. Go on back to your duties."

"I've been run out of me stable as it's being rebuilt."

Gareth gaped up at the man. "Rebuilt?"

"Aye, yer fiancé is having it made into a garage fer her automobiles."

Gareth glowered. "So she's already taking over."

"Aye, it would seem. Wives are known ta do that. Sarah told me ta make sure ye were gettin' ready. I dona think ye can do that down here, and I dona want to get in trouble with the missus."

Gareth had no choice but to allow Thompton to carry him up. He hated that. The man never looked Gareth in the eye when he had to carry him. At least he had that. Thompton sat him in his wingchair.

"Will there be anythin' else?"

"No, thank you."

Thompton bowed before leaving and closing the door behind him.

Gareth hopped up and flew to his trunk. He pulled out the claymore and swung it about to let the tension out. Then he took it in both hands to examine it. "Where did you come from? And what kind of trouble did you bring with you that day?"

There was a quiet knock on Gareth's door.

"Go away."

Whoever it was left, and Gareth continued his swordplay. The only problem in his mind was the question—who was his enemy? Then he thought of Mr. Strong. Who were his friends? Or did he even have any?

Gareth had to figure it out soon. But first he had to gain a wife and do all he could to be rid of her.

Chapter Eleven

Gareth sat in his chair at the bottom of the foyer as the music played. He did his best to smile, but it felt so unnatural, he finally stopped.

Tabitha was the first to descend the stairs in a stylish floral gown, her blonde hair pulled up in an elegant coiffure. She smiled at Gareth as she took her place to the side. Gareth thought about how pretty she looked. The dress was more expensive than any she'd ever worn before. Probably a gift from Jessamine. He wished he could have provided it for her. She deserved to have pretty things and a new life in America. No one there would know her sordid beginnings or care. She'd be foreign and accepted as a lady by Americans impressed by her link to the Kellers, whose daughter would hold an English title. Tabitha would find a respectable husband who adored her and be happy.

He swallowed the emotions which followed that thought. Tabitha was his only companion—the only one in the whole house who had ever fully accepted Gareth. And in two days, she would be gone. He swallowed the thought away. It was selfish. He couldn't hang on to her for his sake. She'd go and be happy, and he would be alone.

The music changed. Everyone stood and turned. Jessamine descended the stairs in a corseted white, lace dress which hugged her figure in all the aesthetically pleasing areas. Gareth's breath caught as his eyes swept over her. She smiled a warm greeting to all the attendants before making eye contact with him. Her dark eyes took on a different appearance when she looked at him. She smiled and bit her lip before a blush flushed her cheeks, and she lowered her gaze to watch him again under long, dark lashes. Gareth had a sense of déjà vu.

Jessamine took her father's arm at the bottom of the stairs, and he escorted her to the altar. She stood beside Gareth's chair and faced the vicar. The ceremony was a blur. Each gave the proper response until Reverend Piper told him to kiss her. Gareth glanced about and then up at Jessamine.

She grinned down before bending toward him. Just when her face was at his, she whispered, "Do not make a spectacle of my wedding. You've behaved so far. I won't attach any meaning to this gesture. So if you so much as flinch, I will make you regret it."

Gareth nodded, trying to make out her words, but the cloud of her warmth and scent made him dizzy. Then her warm, soft lips touched his. He hadn't expected to respond, but without thinking, his hands held her face to his, and he kissed her in return. She stood, and too quickly, it was over. His mind was left a muddle, and his body felt chilled so far from the warmth of hers. The disappointed tug in his gut surprised him as he watched her stand and smile at the guests.

Tabitha rushed toward them, hugging Jessamine first and then Gareth.

Tabitha brushed a loose blonde curl from her blue eyes as she stood. "Gareth, I know you'll be so happy with Jessie once you get to know her. She's perfect for you. I've prayed for you for such a long time, that God would send you someone who could see past the chair and your grumpiness, and He has. She's someone you can be yourself with. I promise. Don't throw this away before giving her a chance."

Gareth wasn't sure how much Tabitha knew about the whole arrangement. He doubted she understood that her new friend was simply after his title, or that his agreement to the marriage was for Tabitha's financial security. She was young, romantic, and naïve, believing her friend truly wanted a love match.

Gareth only smiled at his young aunt. He couldn't crush her belief in happy endings.

Everyone was escorted to the dining hall where Gareth rolled himself up on the dais. Jessamine took her place beside him. She leaned into him and said, "Thank you for not making a scene at the wedding."

Gareth whispered in her ear, "Better to just get the whole bloody thing over with."

Jessamine smiled at him and placed her hand on his. "You are such a romantic."

Dinner was served. While they were eating, Jessamine said in passing, "I want you to know that I respected your wishes today."

Gareth sliced the meat on his plate, not bothering to look at her. "And how did you do that? Did you book your passage back to America with your father?"

"No, when you said, go away...I did."

"What on earth are you talking about?" He concentrated on his bite of ham and avoided looking at her.

"Today I came to tell you something. I'd wanted it out of the way before the wedding, but you wanted to be alone. Now it will have to wait until you're alone in the bedroom with me."

Gareth smirked at her and shook his head. "You are mistaken if you think we will actually be sharing a bedroom."

Jessamine leaned in. "You are mistaken if you think we won't. At least for tonight anyway." She gestured out at the dining hall. "Many of our guests are staying the night.

They had to use my room for another couple. Sarah moved my things over to your room."

Gareth only glared at her in response. He didn't speak to her for the rest of the meal.

The meal gave way to music and chatter. They had not arranged for dancing because of Gareth's condition. It wasn't until later that Gareth broke his silence toward Jessamine, when he saw Mr. Strong take his bride's hand and kiss it. Gareth pushed his chair hard, nearly knocking guests over as he made his way to Mr. Strong and Jessamine.

"Gareth! I was just introducing myself to your lovely bride." The old man grinned wide.

"I'd love to hear some of your stories about Gareth. I'm sure you have many," Jessamine said to the old man and nodded.

"Indeed I do." The old man placed a hand on Gareth's shoulder. "Your bride is enchanting."

Gareth knocked the old man's hand from him. "Yes, she is. Please excuse us." He took Jessamine's hand and led her away.

Jessamine pulled away from him once they were alone in the library. "That was rude."

Gareth scowled at her as he spat out his words. "Don't talk to that man."

Jessamine glowered back at Gareth, placing her hands on her hips. "Why not?"

"I don't…" Gareth choked on the words. "I don't trust him." He swallowed the bile back as he said the words about his former tutor. A man who had helped shape him into an adult.

"But he was your tutor and seemed so genuine and friendly."

"Yes, but I've outgrown tutors so there's no need for any further contact. There's no reason for him to remain in town any longer. He should move back home to his wife."

Jessamine's dark eyes grew into giant, black dots of coal as she glared back at him. "And when we go back out there, what would you have me do? Refuse to speak to the man?"

Gareth glanced at the door. Being in the same room with that man wasn't anything he could stomach at the moment. "We won't go back out there. I've had enough of everyone for the evening. We should retire. Then when we wake, this will all be over." At least the wedding party would be, anyway.

"Not returning would be rude. Won't people think it strange if we don't at least say goodbye?"

Gareth grinned a mischievous smile, "They *will* think it rude of me, but they won't think it *strange* of me."

Jessamine burst into laughter. "I'm sure that's very true. But you don't expect me to be so rude to our guests in the future, do you?"

"I don't expect us to have any guests in the future."

"Well, let me go up first so I can ready myself for bed." Jessamine headed for the door.

Gareth pushed his chair in her way. "No, I will go first. I'll send Tabitha when you can come up."

Jessamine's shoulders sagged in exasperation. "But it's our wedding night. I need to change and prepare myself."

Gareth turned the chair away from her in dismissal. "It's not a real wedding night so don't trouble yourself with any preparation other than that which is needed for sleep."

He wheeled his chair out of the room, leaving Jessamine with what he imagined to be a look of disappointment on her face. Tabitha met him in the corridor.

"Gareth, I was looking for you and Jessamine. Grandfather wants to propose a toast to you both."

"Well, he'll have to do it without us present. Tell him we have retired for the night. Please give everyone our regrets and thank them for attending... blah, blah, blah. You know, the kind of things you would say and I never would. Now help me watch for people so I can get up to my room. Then you can go get Jessamine and send her up."

Tabitha's pink lips grew into the biggest smile. "She's planned the biggest surprise for you. I can't wait to hear about it all tomorrow morning."

Gareth's eyes widened. "I don't feel comfortable talking about this sort of thing with you."

Tabitha giggled as she pushed Gareth behind the stairs and looked about for others. "I'm not talking about what you think I'm talking about, I assure you." She walked the perimeter. "It's all clear."

Gareth escaped up the side of the stairs to the upper floor and went straight for his room. He noticed that Sarah or Thompton had brought in a dressing screen and had placed Jessamine's trunk behind it. He then noticed a hairbrush on the nightstand and perfume beside it. He stood by it and picked up the bottle and sniffed. It was that smell, the one which clouded his thinking.

He quickly changed to his pajamas and climbed into bed. How would they work this out? He couldn't ask a lady to sleep on the floor and blast it if he would give up his bed for the woman. Maybe he *would* tell her to sleep on the floor. Perhaps that could be the end of it all, and she'd leave on her own the next morning.

Jessamine knocked on the door before peeking in. "Is it all right if I enter now?"

"No, but I have no choice in the matter."

She pushed the door closed behind her and looked at the bed, and Gareth in it. "Wow." She swallowed hard. "You're already in bed." Her cheeks flushed as her long lashes fluttered. She bowed her head and bit her lip. "I guess I'll get ready behind that screen."

Gareth picked up a book and pretended to read. "Or go to bed fully dressed if you like. Makes no difference to me." He didn't bother to look at her.

A few moments later, silk rustled and Jessamine's dress appeared, hanging over the screen. He swallowed, and perspiration broke out on his forehead. He shook his head and tried to concentrate on the book in front of him rather than the thought of the beautiful woman disrobing in his room. He could hardly make out the words in the book when he heard her walking toward the bed. He refused to look at her at first.

"I'm just a bit nervous, being in here with you now." A tremor shook her voice.

Gareth glanced up to see Jessamine wrapped in a pink silk dressing gown, almost swaddling herself with it. Her chestnut hair was down around her shoulders, as it had been the night he'd flown her to safety. He was glad she was still fully covered.

"No reason to be nervous. You have slept before, I assume. I promise you, that's all that can possibly happen tonight."

Jessamine's forehead scrunched and wrinkled above her narrowed eyes. "What do you mean?"

"My condition." Gareth motioned to his legs. "There can never be more than a brother-sister relationship between us. Did I not mention that before?" Gareth made an expression of false surprise. "Guess you have grounds for an annulment."

Jessamine shook her head as a mischievous smirk appeared. She sauntered toward him. "I know better than that. Do you remember how we were first introduced? How we met?" She continued to move closer.

Memories of her landing in his lap flashed through his mind. "Yes, you were quite clumsy."

Jessamine's voice grew husky when she stood in front of him. "I found out all I needed to know about the extent of your condition in that very first moment."

Gareth's brows furrowed at first as he tried to understand what she meant. The moment her words sunk in, his mouth hung open at the memory of Jessamine tumbling into his lap and how he'd pushed her out of it, trying not to embarrass himself and her. "You planned that…to find out…?" Gareth glared up at her, his nostrils flared. "No wonder Americans are thought of as crass and ill mannered. No true lady would ever do such a thing."

Jessamine glanced off to the side for just a second. "No, I'm not a true lady. One of the reasons I'm not welcome into the upper echelons of American society. But ladies tend to be stodgy and boring anyway."

She fixed her gaze on Gareth as she moved closer to the bed. Her voice grew husky once again. "You know, refusing me tonight is unlawful. Doesn't scripture say something about not denying your spouse? Something about my body belonging to you and yours to me? I could run down and ask Reverend Piper what the scripture reference is. We were just married before God and family, remember? You made a promise to me in front of them all, and I plan to hold you to it."

Gareth pressed his back into the pillows stacked behind him in an attempt to put space between him and his new bride. She bent over him, her face inches from his. Her warm, sweet breath tickled the skin on his neck, causing goose bumps to pimple there. The floral scent of her perfume addled his brain as usual. He swallowed. "Miss Keller..."

"No, it's Mrs. Smyth now or Lady Smyth if you like. I'm your wife and this is our wedding night. You claim to be a helpless cripple so..." She moved in until their foreheads touched. Gareth could feel the mattress sink where her knee now pressed against his outer thigh. "Maybe I'll take advantage of your helplessness. You say I trapped you. Consider this bed my web and you my fly. Prepare to be devoured."

Gareth couldn't respond, his mind in utter shock. He should make some nasty retort, but there was too much appeal to her threat. He swallowed and tried to speak as she moved in to kiss him. He reached up to brush a strand of hair from her face and leaned in. She was beautiful.

Just as their lips were about to meet, Jessamine was up in an instant and off the bed, walking toward the balcony. "But taking advantage of your helplessness would be wrong of me...very, very wrong. If you don't want me in that way, I just need to accept it and respect your wishes."

Gareth shook his head and struggled to speak, "But...What?" was all that he could manage, his mind still addled. His breaths came in whispered pants, and he swallowed. Had the room grown warm, or was it just him?

Jessamine reached into the pocket of her dressing gown. "I got you a wedding gift. I wanted to give it to you earlier today and talk to you about it, but you didn't grant me admittance."

She traipsed back to the bed and handed him the small, wrapped box. "I used to have two of these, but I lost one as a child, on a trip to visit my aunt... at least that's what I told my mother. In truth, I left the other with someone as a thank you." She backed away. "I'm going out on the balcony for air. When you open it, if you have questions...you will know where to find me." Her smile was shy before she turned and stepped out the balcony door.

Gareth stared after her, desperately calming himself. Once he finally got himself together, he opened the box. Inside was a small blue-green stone. It was smooth and looked almost identical to the one he had. Gareth's breath caught. He stared out the door of the balcony. He leaned over to his nightstand and yanked the drawer open. He pulled out the stone he'd had since childhood and held the two together. They nearly matched in size and were identical in color.

Gareth swallowed. "Miss Keller?"

No answer.

"I mean Mrs...oh bother...Jessamine? Come in here immediately. Explain the meaning of this gift. I need to know where you got this stone."

Jessamine didn't answer. Gareth flew to just behind the door and stood in the doorway, peering out. "Jessamine?" He glanced around the door out onto the balcony, but she wasn't there.

"Jessamine?" He flew out onto the balcony, glancing in every direction. It was small with no place to hide. Her dressing gown puddled on the floor.

Where had she gone? Gareth looked out into the darkness. She said if he had questions, he'd know where to find her...and he did.

Chapter Twelve

She was the girl at the tree. Gareth stood and blinked into the darkness, unsure about what to do next. The cold air wicked away the sweat from his forehead. *She knew.* His throat tightened as he swallowed this realization. He needed to talk to her *now* and find out the extent of her knowledge. She had shown up around the same time as the attacks. Was she involved in that as well? Gareth peered out into the darkness and was so tempted to just go after her, but he couldn't risk being seen flying about. The armor. He quickly shook himself out of the daze and made his way to his trunk. He donned his armor before darting into the night sky.

The lights from the house and the noise of wedding guests filled the night. They were still inside enjoying the party he and Jessamine had left early. He clung to the shadows of trees as he made his way through the yard.

Was she really the girl from his childhood? If so, who else had she told? Did her father know? Had she told others? He'd been so careful with his secret, sharing it only with the person he trusted most, Tabitha. He hardly knew the woman who was now his wife. Could she be trusted? Was she in with Mr. Strong?

His breath caught when he got to the oak tree and found her perched on a limb. Gareth landed and stood under the tree, looking up at her.

Jessamine's eyes remained looking in the distance while she said, "So we meet again, Flying Knight, I told my husband about meeting you, but he treated me as if I were daft." Jessamine looked back at Gareth before grinning with one eyebrow raised. "He was so convincing that it made me question what I knew."

Gareth was at a loss for words. He swallowed and glanced around, making sure they were alone. Anger rattled his words as he spoke them slowly through gritted teeth, "And what exactly is it that you think you know? Who else have you told?"

Jessamine put her palm against the trunk of the tree and pursed her lips just before speaking. "I was hoping to meet my husband here instead of you, but I guess you'll do. I need him to know that I didn't come here to wed an English lord. I came here looking for the boy who saved me as a child. I was here before when I was seven, visiting my aunt, and climbed this very tree. I asked a boy in a wheelchair to keep watch for me. I was always getting into mischief back then. I drove my mother mad with worry." She gazed at him through narrowed eyes and smirked. "I still do actually." She shook her head and continued. "Anyway, the limb broke, and I was falling until suddenly, I wasn't."

Jessamine released the trunk, balancing herself on the limb. It was then Gareth noticed what she had on; a black, long-sleeved blouse with a black corset hugging it to her at the bodice, black trousers, and high black boots.

"The boy was flying. Other than you, I've not met another person who can. I've never been able to shake the boy or the thrilling sensation of flight. In my mind, he has always been the most handsome and most noble young man of my acquaintance. When it came time to marry, no man trapped by gravity would do." Her eyes widened with excitement as she stared into his face. "And then you flew me to safety the other night, and it was even more exhilarating than I remembered, perhaps because you flew me around longer than the first time. Not that the arrows didn't frighten me, but I trusted you would keep me safe."

Gareth stood as a statue. The gears of his mind worked itself into a jumbled mess. "Who else have you told this story to? Are you cohorts with the person who attacked us? Or do you expect me to think that a coincidence?"

Her eyes narrowed, and her jaw hardened. "No one. Not ever. You think I had some part in the attack?"

"You showed up and so did the attacker. What else am I to think?"

She shook her head vigorously. "I was just as surprised as you the other night. I came here looking for the boy who saved me. My parents put pressure on me to find a husband. They kept setting me up to meet nice gentlemen back in America, but all I could think of was the boy...you. I couldn't exactly tell them why I wanted to come here in search for a husband, so I led them to believe I wanted a man of title."

Jessamine glared at him. "I'm being completely honest with you about who I am. I think that honesty is paramount to a marriage. I want you to feel as safe with me as I do with you. Know I will do all I can to protect your secret."

She glanced about in the darkness around them as if she too were making sure they were alone. "I've been fascinated with the idea of flight ever since we first met. There are a couple of brothers back in the states who have been working on flying, using some giant contraption, but I desire a more personal experience." Jessamine bit her lip. "So I, too, have been working on flight."

Her hand fluttered up, and she pulled a string on her corset. Gears began clicking in time as a layer of the black corset unfolded and spread out into wings. Jessamine smiled.

"Here goes," she shouted and jumped from the tree.

Gareth lurched forward to leap up and catch her, but he realized she really was flying. She circled the space between the limb and the ground until she landed directly in front of Gareth. She pulled another string and again the clicking of gears sounded as the wings retracted. Gareth bent to the side in one direction and then another, trying to get a better view of the strange corset and where the gears could be hiding. As tightly as it cinched her waist, they had to be the most minute of gears.

He circled her, bending closer to get a better look at the garment usually worn under women's clothing. He couldn't ignore the fact that the breeches gave him a better look at her figure than the pretty dresses ever had, and he had to swallow. Then he caught her floral scent and stood up straight. The assault on his more basic nature as a man wasn't helping him think clearly.

Before he could speak, she did. "So are you going to return the favor and show me who you really are? Tell me if my deduction is correct? Can we start this marriage as our true selves?"

Gareth hesitated, not sure if he could trust her. In one quick motion he moved forward and grabbed her up in his arms, taking flight. "Not here."

Jessamine clung to him as they flew back to the house. She giggled and pulled away, jerking the cord again and releasing her wings. She stretched out, only holding Gareth's hand, letting her wings hold her up alongside him.

They reached the yard moments later. The wedding guests had made their way home or to their rooms for the most part, with only the servants seen through the gas-lit windows of Waverly Park. Gareth, again, made sure no one saw them as he landed on his balcony. He released his embrace of her as soon as her feet touched the floor. His flight continued into their room, and he landed at a distance, at first facing away, not sure he could follow through with it. He swallowed hard and turned back to face Jessamine.

She stood in the doorway and pulled the string which started another series of gear clicks. Her wings retracted, and she stepped into the room. Watching her with her hair loose about her face, falling down to her waist, her cheeks pink from the night air—she was lovely. He remembered the girl who spoke to him under the tree as a child. She'd not been frightened by his wheelchair as the others had been. She'd seen him, not the chair. Maybe she still saw him that way.

Gareth considered his bride, the mysterious woman he hardly knew, who had pursued him as a suitor. He'd thought it over and didn't think she was part of the attacks. She'd been genuinely frightened that night the arrows chased them. But then again, he'd trusted Mr. Strong as well. Either way, she already knew the truth about him. He nodded and did something he thought he would never do around anyone but Tabitha. His hands took hold of the cold iron on both sides of his face, and he removed his helmet.

Jessamine moved closer, her dark eyes wide and moist with emotion. She placed her right hand on his bare cheek. "Thank you."

Gareth suddenly questioned his actions and bolted away from her. His heart accelerated. He'd never imagined he'd have someone to share his secret with. The newness of it frightened him. He chose anger to fill in the blanks, as always, trying to figure out how to handle the situation. He turned on her and injected his words with venom. "Who have you told? You want me to believe you've really never told anyone else? That you and the attacker showing up at the same time is just coincidence?"

Jessamine turned and looked up under long, dark lashes. "I've spoken with Tabitha, but only because we sort of figured out that we both already knew."

Gareth crossed his arms over his chest. Doubt caused his voice to quiver. "And no one else? Not your father or your mother? Not even as a child when it happened?"

Jessamine shook her head. "No one, I promise." She moved closer. "I know what it is to keep secrets, to hide who you truly are. I'm expected to be a silly, frivolous girl, thinking only of pretty lace and the next party. Smart women, women who have a mind and want to use it, are shunned by society. Tabitha told me that here they are called bluestockings as an insult." She stood directly in front of Gareth. Her dark eyes searched his for understanding. "I was hoping, after tonight, we could both feel free to be ourselves around each other. I don't want to hide at home, and I want my home to be with you."

Jessamine moved closer, kissing Gareth softly on the lips before backing away too quickly for Gareth's hungry mind.

She'd really kept his secret all these years. Perhaps it was the idea of having someone he could trust after all which caused him to believe her. Or maybe it was the way she looked at him which made him want to take hold of her and pull her back to him, but all the uncertainty, the unknown of it all, engulfed him. "I never thought I would be able to share this other part of myself with anyone...or any of myself for that matter." As he spoke the words, he realized this could end up being a very true marriage after all. The idea excited and frightened him at once.

Jessamine's lips turned up a bit, but in a suppressed manner, before she spoke. "I have so many questions. I'm afraid I'll blurt them all out at once and ruin everything with my babble. Can you tell me *how* you fly? Is it something you were born with? Have you always been able to do it? I ask because you looked almost as shocked as I felt the day I fell from the tree."

Gareth kept his face blank as he remembered, "I was. It was the first time for me. Seeing you fall seemed to trigger it."

Jessamine walked to the opposite wall and leaned her back against it. "Nice to know I was your first." She glanced up under dark lashes again, her cheeks blushing pink as she bit her bottom lip.

Did she need to always flirt and stir up his thoughts into a jumbled mess? Gareth glanced away and clenched his jaw tight. He needed to think on what they were discussing instead of how it would feel to suddenly crash into Jessamine, pin her against the wall and taste her lips, her tongue, her chin, her neck and...

He shook the thoughts from his head and looked at her again since looking away wasn't helping. He wasn't ready to share everything. "I understand you came back here looking for the boy who saved you. I also understand you thought it might be me. What I don't understand is that you still pursued me after speaking with me."

"Really? Why is that?" She grinned and tilted her head.

Gareth rolled his eyes. "I'm known to be quite rude and difficult."

Jessamine giggled, lighting her face and eyes with a knowing smile. "Really? I hadn't noticed."

"If you didn't, it means I need to work harder at your talents of perception."

She was clever. Gareth could tell by her expressions that there was a lot going on inside her head, and it intrigued him as much as her pretty face. He was so enraptured by her, he hardly noticed the sound of the wind moving the balcony door just slightly.

Jessamine pushed up from the wall and sauntered toward him. She reached up and knocked her balled fist against his armor. "I knew your surly attitude was like this armor, something to keep people from knowing who you really are. Protection from getting hurt. Only you don't need either with me." She pushed up on her toes and wrapped her arms around Gareth's neck, bringing his lips to hers. This wasn't a quick sisterly peck as before.

He encircled her with his arms, pulling her closer, wishing the hard armor wasn't between them so he could feel her soft body pressed against his. Her lips were sweet as he took the kiss deeper. He was contemplating what to do next. After all, it was his wedding night.

A crash sounded behind him, and he was nearly knocked over as two small bodies ran into his legs. He barely caught Jessamine as she started to fall.

"What the devil?" Gareth shouted. He pulled back from Jessamine. Tabitha's dog and cat raced past the two of them. Patches, the cat, leapt onto the bed before springing with a wild growl out toward the balcony. The tabby landed on a man dressed in dark clothing hiding in the shadows. Rory growled, lunged, and sunk his teeth into the man's calf.

Gareth stepped in front of Jessamine and drew his claymore, readying himself. He hoped all his training with Mr. Strong had been sufficient since he'd never actually engaged anyone in a real fight. His mind raced as he wondered how long the man had been there. What had he heard?

But the animals' momentum had the invader at the edge of the balcony and falling over it before Gareth could fully gather his thoughts.

"Stay here." Gareth grabbed his helmet and pushed it onto his head before flying down to investigate. When he got to the lawn, there wasn't anyone there, not even the animals. He glanced around before kneeling to see if there was any sign of which way they had gone. A thud sounded behind him. He spun around, a hand on the hilt of his sword, only to find Jessamine standing there. "I told you to stay put."

"But I wanted to help. Who was that?"

"I don't know. Fly back up and bolt the window and door until I get back. He could be armed and you aren't wearing armor."

"Number one, I can't fly up. I can only glide down. Second, the fabric of my outfit is a special weave my mother designed for the military. She doesn't just innovate the production of textiles; she's been working on the fabrics, too." She pulled at the puffy sleeve of her shirt. "This is as tough as chainmail with a double layer of it around my bodice where vital organs are." She shrugged. "I've always been a bit of a tomboy, falling out of trees and such. It worried my mother, thus she originally designed the fabric for me. When I decided to try and fly, she made me this flight suit."

Gareth was about to argue when she interrupted him. "Look, I'm not the sit-at-home, prettying-my-hair type. Another pair of eyes and a working brain can't hurt in trying to find out who is after you."

He sighed and reached out to push a strand of Jessamine's hair behind her ear. "Your head is still unprotected. We wouldn't want your pretty face and highly intelligent mind damaged by an arrow."

"You think I'm pretty?" Jessamine reached behind her back and pulled out a stocking cap. "I have this, and it's made of the same fabric. It's not very sexy, but I will wear it if it means I can come." She pulled the black mask over her head and down to the top of her nose. There was a cutout for her eyes. "Let's be off now because the man is either getting away or being eaten by your house pets. Let's go find out which, shall we?"

Chapter Thirteen

Gareth grabbed Jessamine's hand, and they took flight. The clear sky was full of stars, and the nearly full moon ruled the night. On the horizon was one lone, dark cloud that struck him as odd since it sat so low in the ether. He stared for a moment.

"Did you see where they went?" Jessamine broke through his thoughts. "And how did the dog and cat know?"

He blinked hard and met her eyes. He had wondered that, too. "I don't know."

"Which? Where they went or about your intuitive pets?"

"Neither. I don't see a trail in any direction. Not even a spot where they might have landed. I don't think the man did. Whoever attacked us tonight can fly as well."

Jessamine's breath caught. "Someone else able to fly?"

"I don't have to worry about you running off with him, do I? We English hate scandal."

"I'm not so singular about flying that any man who can conquer the sky will do. I wanted a particular man who could fly." She grew silent as if thinking for a moment before continuing. "Do your pets also fly?"

Gareth shook his head. "I don't know. They've never done anything of the sort before."

"If you don't know where they went, where are we going?"

"To Mr. Strong's house."

"Why there?"

"I have my suspicions about him. After the last attack, his house remained lit up until the early morning hours. The next day, his house was ransacked, blood pooled on the floor, and Mr. Strong missing. When he returned, he acted as though nothing had happened."

"So, that is the reason you wanted me away from him at the wedding. I wondered why you had transcended even your own normal rudeness with him."

"I thought he'd been harmed because of his association with me. If he can fly, as I suspect, he probably knows more about me than I do. My plan was to send everyone away after the wedding and fire the staff so no one would be in danger while I got to the bottom of it all."

"How did you plan to get rid of me?"

"By being my normal, charming self."

"You would have failed there. I made my vow before God and man. I'm not going anywhere."

He glanced her way. She shot him her flirty smile. He grimaced.

Everyone left him eventually.

They landed just outside Mr. Strong's house. The glow of lamplight peeked around the curtains in the window.

"Stay here."

Gareth flew as hard as he could through the front door of the house, pushing it off the hinges as he entered. He glanced up, and his mouth hung open at what he saw. A man he didn't recognize was tied to a chair. Long, greasy, black bangs fell into the man's dark, sunken eyes. A vein under the pale skin of his temple protruded and pulsed. He wore all black, and one of his lips was split and bleeding. Sarah and Thompton circled him.

"What the bloody hell is going on? What are you two doing here? Where is Mr. Strong?"

Jessamine came running through the door, stopping just behind Gareth. "What are the maid and manservant doing here?"

Sarah clasped her hands and smiled. "Look at that. He knows 'bout her and brought her along. A fine match indeed. I told ye the court'll be in good hands with the two of 'em."

The man bound to the chair spit. "Their offspring will be more human than Fae. I pledge no fealty to human filth."

Sarah lifted her hand across her body before bringing the back of it hard against the man's face. "Ye speak treason against our king and queen. Ye better recant because the penalty fer that be death. Now, I'll be askin' ye again, who sent ye?"

"The true king sent me. One of pure blood. Na the filthy abomination ye seek to put on the throne."

Thompton stepped in between his wife and their prisoner. He bent over the man in the chair and placed a dagger to the man's throat. "Ye'll be spillin' yer guts or we'll be spillin'em fer ye."

Gareth shouted again. "Where is Mr. Strong?"

Sarah spun to face him. "Lord Smyth, we'll be answerin' all yer questions as soon as we finish with him."

She turned back to the man. "Yer kind don't even belong to our court. Yer Unseelie. Who are ye to be callin' humans filth. Ye feed off their misery."

The man in the chair stuck out his chin in an act of pride and defiance. Sweat beaded his forehead, and his dark eyes blazed. "The true king will unite the two courts. Bringin' the strengths of both the Seelie and Unseelie together to form the most powerful Fae court there ever has been or ever will be. Humanity will hide from us, and na the other way around. I sacrifice me self for this glorious cause."

Thompton stood behind the man. "By the power granted to me by King Tristan of the Seelie Court of Ansleigh, God rest his soul, I pronounce ye guilty of attempting to assassinate the rightful heir to the Seelie throne. Have ye anything to say for yerself?"

Two drops of sweat trickled from the man's forehead into his narrowed, dark eyes. He blinked the perspiration away. "The line of Ansleigh died with his whore daughter's betrayal of the court. I serve the true King."

"And who is yer true King?" Thompton asked, pressing the knife into the man's throat.

Suddenly, the man raised his head and flung his Adam's apple onto the knife, sending it deep into his flesh. Blood spilt out around the hilt of the knife and over Thompton's hand. The man's dark eyes met Gareth's with a defiant light which faded slowly as the life drained away.

Gareth looked away as Jessamine turned into him, but the sound of the man's gurgling last breaths could not be kept out of their ears.

Sarah broke the silence, her voice quiet and somber. "Well, he was loyal to the false king to the end, just like the others. We still have no idea who be after the throne." She turned to them with distressed eyes. "Allow us to clean up this mess, and we will answer all yer questions, Lord Gareth."

The two servants Gareth had thought he'd known for years started their work. He thought he'd known them, but as they drew knives from their belts and began the task, he felt he watched strangers. They worked with the utmost efficiency to unbind the man's body from the chair, laid him on the rug, and rolled him up in it.

"Wish we'd had a rug last time. The rug was a grand idea, sweetings," Sarah said to Thompton as they gathered the ends and headed for the backdoor with the man's body.

Jessamine removed her stocking cap and leaned into Gareth. "Did you know your housekeepers were capable of this?"

Gareth pulled off his helmet, deciding there was no point in it at the moment since it seemed they already knew who he was. His mind felt blank. "Not a clue."

A few moments later, the two were back, only this time they were flying, buzzing about the room putting the furniture to right. Once the door was returned to its hinges, they called Gareth and Jessamine to the settee and stood in front of them.

Sarah grinned, "Would ye care fer some tea before we get started?"

Thompton, who was already seated in the wingback chair, pulled Sarah down to sit on the armrest. "They just watched us interrogate a man and dispose of the body. They'll not be interested in tea." Thompton directed his attention to

Gareth. "Ye have questions, I'm sure, lad. Go ahead and ask them."

Gareth's heart raced as a million questions, both new and old, filled his mind. "Where is Mr. Strong?"

"Long dead. Killed by me spice cake on that first visit. The spices were enchanted to kill anyone with plans to harm ye. The moment he started choking, we knew he was an enemy. We just didna know who had sent him. I'm sure ye noticed I fed that cake whenever we had company. We needed to check anyone who was to come in close contact to ye." She grinned at Jessamine. "Even to ye. But I could tell early on, ye'd be good fer Lord Tristan."

"Then who has been tutoring me all these years?"

"That was me." Thompton leaned forward. "I'd been looking fer a way to start makin' ye ready to take the throne fer years, but having the role of stable hand never gave me opportunity. As yer tutor, I could teach ye everything ye'd need to be ready when King Tristan passed, God rest his soul. We knew with the loss of his wife and daughter, he'd not be around much longer."

Gareth shook his head. "Who is King Tristan, and how have you passed as Mr. Strong? Some kind of sorcery?"

Sarah smiled. "Nay, na sorcery. Thompton and I are mimics or changelings. We can take the shape of any living thing we choose, both man and beast." She glanced at Thompton. "Let's show him how we best kept tabs on him and those in the house."

He nodded, and with a swirl of air and a flash of light, Tabitha's cat and dog stood where they once were. In another swirl and flash, they returned shape to Thompton and Sarah.

Jessamine pointed at Sarah. "That's how you knew about me. You were always with us in the bonnet room."

"Aye, I loved seeing you girls getting' close and whisperin' your praises of our Lord Tristan. He's such a handsome boy with a good heart. Ye could see it, and it warmed me heart toward ye, even if yer na Fae."

"Is that why I can fly? I'm Fae? And you keep calling me Tristan and named a King Tristan."

Sarah smiled. "Aye, yer Fae by yer mother, well, half-Fae. But yer as fair of heart as any whole Fae could be, even more than some. Yer mother placed ye in me arms herself and asked me to watch over ye. And I have. Her father was King Tristan, of the Seelie Court of Ansleigh."

"My mother's name was Ansleigh."

Thompton shook his head. "Yer mother's name was Princess Seyraed of the Court of Ansleigh. She sold her birthright to an Unseelie sorceress to make your father enamored with her, but she took the name as her first. I think it was a way to preserve some part of her birthright. King Tristan saw it as she sold *her* birthright, but not yers. He sent us to watch over ye and keep ye safe until time to take the throne. When the claymore arrived, we knew our sovereign was no more. Ye be our king."

Then Sarah and Thompton, together, fell to their knees and bowed. "We are at yer service, King Tristan the second, of the Seelie Court of Ansleigh."

Chapter Fourteen

Gareth stared at his house servants kneeling before him, their words and actions sinking in. In an instant, he pulled away from Jessamine and leapt back, hovering on the other side of the room. "I'm no king. Stand up, now—this instant! I demand it!"

Sarah stood first. "Ye very much be our king, grandson of King Tristan the first. He and his nephew, Tinkton, assigned us to yer protection and trainin' when ye were just a wee lad. We've done our job to ready ye fer this day and now it's here. The Court of Ansleigh's claymore was delivered to yer door pronouncin' ye the new king."

Gareth shook his head, his eyes wide with fury. "I don't want it. I don't know anything about being a king or being Fae. I'm the crippled grandson of a penniless lord whose only wish, my entire life, has been to be left alone. Find yourself another king because I'm not him."

Thompton stood and moved to his wife's side. He brushed a hand through his brown hair. "There be no one else. Ye be the heir. If ye don't return to the Seelie Court of Ansleigh with us, we will be overthrown by whoever it be trying to kill ye and claim the throne. And dona think by turning away from yer birthright and yer calling that ye will na be in danger. Whoever the false king be, he willna stop 'til he be sure ye are out of the way. He'll na leave any chance fer ye to change yer mind and come after the throne. As far as what ye know or dona know about being king, I've taught ye a great deal and will continue helping ye, if ye allow it."

Gareth only considered the man silently.

Thompton shifted his weight from one foot to the other and then hovered just above the floor. "Yer a natural protector. That's yer instincts from yer Fae half. Ye dona see the elder Lord Smyth concerned about the people of the village. When ye were just a lad, ye knew ye had to save a girl falling from a tree. I watched ye from me porch. Then later, ye felt it yer duty to protect the townsfolk from vandals. Yer meant to protect the people under ye, just not here in this shire."

Jessamine moved to where Gareth hovered. Her face had lost color, and her wide eyes showed she was as stunned as he was. She took his arm protectively and spoke to the couple. "I think this is a bit much for all at once, don't you?

Perhaps we should go home and get some rest and discuss it further tomorrow. The decision doesn't have to be made at this moment."

Gareth's chin jutted out. "There's nothing more to discuss now or tomorrow."

Sarah nodded in agreement before turning to Thompton. "It's their wedding night. We should send them home and talk more about it when Lord Smyth, Tabitha, and the guests be gone."

Gareth replaced the helmet on his head and pulled Jessamine to him. This was too much, and he'd had enough. He headed for the door.

Thompton blocked their exit. "Sir, I'm afraid I can't let ye leave alone. We will escort yer majesty and yer bride back to Waverly Park. After two attempts on yer life in one week, we can't allow ye to travel about at night by yerself."

Heat rose to Gareth's cheeks. *How dare he?* Gareth hated the idea of an escort when all he wanted was the freedom to be alone. He shook his head and spoke through clenched teeth. "I can handle things myself, thank you."

The worried look in Thompton's eyes gave him pause. And the man servant held out a hand with a slightly bowed head.

"Mi'lord, I know ye be very capable and strong. After all, I had a hand in yer trainin'. But the Unseelie fairies be cunning and harbor knowledge of the dark arts. If ye and the lady were to be attacked, it would be far better that the four of us were at hand to defend."

Gareth swallowed. The man was right. He didn't know anything about how to fight Unseelie fairies should he and Jessamine be attacked. It seemed he knew no one, not even himself. People he thought he knew were not as they seemed and neither was he. Sarah and Thompton had been in his household his whole life, and he never realized anything was off about them. Mr. Strong wasn't even real.

With a nod he acquiesced, more out of numbed shock and simmering irritations than true agreement. Thompton led the group from the house, motioning to Gareth when it was clear for him and Jessamine to follow. Jessamine released her wings upon exiting the door while Sarah took the rear of the group. The four of them traveled over the darkest parts of the fields and forests back to the estate and onto Gareth's balcony. Sarah and Thompton checked the room over, looking behind furniture, curtains, and under the bed, before heading for the hallway.

Thompton turned and faced them. "I'll be taking first watch by the door in the form of Rory, the dog. Sarah will take second watch. We've bolted the balcony entrance. We ask yer Highness not to step foot on it tonight."

Jessamine smiled at Thompton as she padded toward him. "Thank you, Mr. Thompton. We will remain in for the night."

Once Sarah and Thompton exited, Gareth landed in the chair, ripped off his helmet, and tossed it to the floor. It clattered with a loud thud as it bounced off the hardwood floor.

Jessamine sauntered to the footrest in front of him and took a seat. "Not quite the wedding night I had in mind."

Gareth said nothing, his mind overflowing with thoughts. He had no interest in being King of the Fae. All he'd ever sought was to be left alone. Now he was not only saddled with a wife he never wanted, but a kingdom and a couple of bodyguards he realized had napped in his lap from time to time. The whole thing was ridiculous. He had a mind to turn them all out of his house and lock himself away from the madness.

When Gareth refused to acknowledge her, Jessamine stood. "I'm going to ready myself for bed. Perhaps you should do the same." She made her way to the screen where she had changed just hours earlier.

Gareth stood and pulled off his armor while she was dressing. His mind wasn't on what he was doing or the change to his sleeping arrangements. He climbed into bed in his underclothes rather than his nightshirt.

Jessamine came around the screen, again in her dressing gown, only this time it was open and revealed a satin crème gown with pink lace. His breath caught. The top of the gown was open, and the thin lace barely hid her accompaniments. He glanced away when she removed her robe and climbed into bed beside him. Gareth swallowed and quickly reached out and turned down the lamp to hide in the darkness. He turned in the bed and faced away from Jessamine, hoping that not seeing her would help. But her scent and warmth were enough to stir up his already muddled mind.

"Tomorrow, I think you should return home with your father."

The bed shifted as she bolted up. "What?"

His voice cracked, so he hardened it. "It's not safe here for you. You won your personal quest to find me, the boy who saved you. Let that be enough of a victory for you and go back to America with Tabitha and your father. My life has become a jumbled tale from the Brothers Grimm, and there's really no place in it for a wife."

Gareth heard her feet slap the floor as she stomped her way to his side of the bed. She turned up the gas lamp when she got there. Her face screwed into a pout as she spoke in a harsh whisper. "What do you mean there's no place for me in your life right now? I've promised to be with you through good and bad, and I take my vows seriously."

The amount of flesh showing along the laced top of her gown made it difficult to remember what he was going to say. He shut his eyes as if to try to sleep. "I don't remember attempted assassination by evil fairies being in the vows. Now please turn the lamp down, and let's get to sleep. It's been a long day, and you've got to get up and pack in the morning."

178

Jessamine shoved at Gareth's shoulder. "You don't get to decide if I'm leaving. I decide if and when I ever leave. And I'm telling you now—I'm not going."

"You also vowed to obey me. The decision's made." Gareth pulled his pillow from below his head and placed it over his face.

Jessamine yanked the pillow from him and threw it across the room, hitting a mirror on the wall and tilting it askew. "I thought we were making progress before the assassin showed up. What's going on in your head? I don't understand."

Gareth sprang up from the bed and retrieved his pillow, trying to avoid eye contact with her. "The problem is you've made all kinds of assumptions about me. Some proved true, so you think you've got me figured out. In your mind, I've secretly been pushing people away when all the while I've wanted something else. The truth is, I like my life of isolation. I'm not interested in more. I don't want anyone around who depends on me. All I want is to be left alone. So if you care so much about my happiness, you can leave on the boat which brought you here."

Jessamine stood upright, staring back at Gareth. Her lip quivered, and her dark eyes shone with unshed tears. "But you kissed me. We were talking like normal people before the pets came crashing in."

Gareth flew to the bed and placed his pillow on it. He took a breath and steadied himself before turning to face her.

"You're a beautiful woman, and you're alone with me in my room. I reacted to it. I'm still capable of reacting to *that* if you want a more *normal* wedding night. But a kiss or even making love doesn't mean I have any more feelings for you now than I had yesterday. Earlier, I was shocked to learn you knew my secret, and it threw me. Now, I don't wish to discuss it any further tonight. I'm tired, and I just want to sleep."

Gareth threw himself into his bed and pulled the covers over his head. No one was going to assume they knew him or what he should do with his life. He had a plan before the wedding to send everyone away, and he would stick to it. He didn't owe anyone anything. And with that he reached up and turned the lamp down, leaving Jessamine to stand alone in the dark.

He tucked himself into his blanket, convinced the conversation was over. He expected some kind of sniveling from the corner where he heard her creep off to, but there wasn't any such sound. His heart sank at the thought that he'd hurt her, but he sucked in a deep breath, convinced it was for the best. There were too many unknowns in his future. Unseelie Fae assassins were trying to kill him, and Seelie Faes were trying to drag him back to their court and make him king.

Gareth flipped onto his back. He was in no position to protect her, not the way a good husband should, and how could he even hope to be a good husband? He'd never seen one before. Well, there was Thompton but he hardly knew the man...er...fairy.

Gareth flipped over to his other side now that Jessamine was no longer in the bed. The cool cotton sheet no longer held her body heat. He breathed in. *Ugh. Her scent was still there.*

Her scent always made it hard to stay angry. The memory of her warm body inches from him flooded his mind along with the ache that she wouldn't be there any longer. He reached out to touch the spot when water splashed over him, drenching him, the blankets, and bed.

Gareth bolted up. His eyes locked on Jessamine's silhouette standing with the pitcher from the wash stand. He wiped the water from his face. "What the devil?"

Jessamine lowered the jug and shifted her hip to the side. "If I can't sleep, neither will you. And I'm not going anywhere. That *is* the final decision. "

With that she slammed the pitcher down on the nightstand and stomped off to the other side of the room.

Chapter Fifteen

Gareth and Jessamine didn't speak the remainder of the night. He'd folded the blanket to form a pallet from the parts which weren't soaked, while she rested in the chair. Crickets chirped through the night, and the moon cut through the slit in the curtains with a silvery glow. The lonely sounds of constant repositioning came and went, but no sleep was to be had by either of the newlyweds.

When the early morning calls of birds replaced that of the crickets, a soft knock came to the door. "Are ye decent? I've got yer breakfast." Sarah poked her head in before she entered with the tray. "I've made excuses fer ye with the extra guests that ye were sleepin' in and wished them all safe travel."

Sarah pushed open the curtains, letting warm golden sun illuminate the bed chamber before turning and gasping at the room in shambles. "What in heaven's name?" She glanced between the two of them as she spoke. "Ye were gettin' on so well last evenin' until the assassin." She stormed over to the bed. "And why is the bed soaked?"

Gareth no longer bothered with pretense. He flew to the table where she'd placed the tray and poured himself some coffee. He did his best to gulp the hot liquid energy without burning his tongue. "She poured water on me because I was trying to sleep when she wanted to argue."

Sarah chuckled. "I'd forgotten this part of being newly married." She bit back a smile as she began tidying up the room.

Jessamine strode toward Sarah, flailing her arms toward Gareth. "How can he sleep when we have such a big problem between us?"

Sarah turned to face her. "I don't know, sweeting, but it seems to be normal for men to just roll over and sleep while we are still screamin' at 'em. Now eat up so I can help ye with yer corset. Tabitha's been circlin' a big box sent here as a wedding gift. She hears tickin' and is dyin' to find out what it be."

Jessamine marched to the table, grabbing a bread roll as she headed for the screen. "Oh, I don't need help with my corset. Mine are all self-lacing."

Sarah tilted her head, her brows furrowed. "Self-lacing?"

"Yes, another creation from my mother. You pull a string and gears cinch it to your chosen tightness. Tell Tabitha we'll be right down."

"Yes, milady." Sarah nodded and left the room.

Gareth made his way to his bureau and quickly dressed before Jessamine could come out from behind the screen. When she emerged, she was put together in a stylish, garnet day dress and ruffled, black bustle. Dark ringlets fell about her hair bun.

She tilted her head just so she could glance up under dark lashes. "Shall I go first to make sure you can fly down?"

Gareth sighed. "I suppose that is necessary with your father and Grandfather still in the house."

Jessamine headed for the door and paused. "You want to send me away even though I know your secret?"

Gareth shook his head. "You've kept it this long...I suppose I can trust you'll continue to keep it."

"See, you admit you can trust me. How many people can you say that about? Does it really mean nothing to you?"

Gareth clenched his jaw. He was caught off guard and had no reply.

"Not only can you trust me but know that I am a woman who finds you extraordinary."

Gareth rolled his eyes with a look of disinterest. "Because I can fly."

Jessamine moved closer. "No, not because of that one thing, but because of who you are."

"And how do you know who I am when I don't even know?"

She positioned herself in front of him to make eye contact. "Because I can see you. I always could. Even before I knew you could fly, remember? If you let me into your life, I'll help you see it, too."

"Maybe you see only what you want to see."

She shook her head as her shoulders fell. "I'll whistle when it's clear."

She left, and Gareth took a breath to clear his head. But, as usual, it didn't work when the room was full of Jessamine's essence. A soft whistle came, and he zipped out the door and down over the stair's railing, landing in his chair. Jessamine stepped behind him to push it.

"I can manage," Gareth snapped.

Jessamine stepped away and put up her hands in surrender. "As you wish."

They made their way to the study where Tabitha circled a giant, white box with a lavender bow on top holding it together. The box was the size of a wardrobe.

"Finally, you two are down. This arrived an hour ago, and I'm just dying to find out what's in it. I hear ticks and clicks. I'm wondering if it's from someone in the bonnet club."

Gareth glanced away bored. "Perhaps it holds the world's largest bonnet."

Jessamine and Tabitha only giggled and made knowing glances at each other.

"Who does it say it's from?" Jessamine asked as she moved closer to inspect it.

"It doesn't. But I'd wager it something very modern."

Jessamine stepped back and stood next to Gareth. She set a soft hand on his shoulder. He relented and let it stay. Her eyes twinkled at him, and then she nodded to Tabitha. "Go ahead. Pull the ribbon."

Tabitha squealed, jumping around in her blue day dress, making her loose blonde curls bounce. She pulled the ribbon, and the sides of the box fell away to reveal a tall, silver horse. Steam escaped its nostrils.

Jessamine clapped her hands in delight. "It's beautiful."

Gareth wheeled his chair around to inspect it from a different angle. "What is it?"

Tabitha circled the metallic animal, rubbing her hand along the body. "It's a steam horse. It's part of the women's underground movement."

Gareth circled back in the other direction. "The what?"

Jessamine pulled out her charm necklace to show Gareth. "It's a small underground movement headed by women to modernize society. It's like a secret sisterhood. Our charms show other women of the movement that we too are part of it. We have an owl charm to symbolize wisdom, a gear to show we are mechanizing, a clock to show we are women of the times, and individual charms for our special interest of knowledge. See, I have wings."

Tabitha continued to circle the horse. "But if it's steam-powered, why do I hear the clicking and whirring of clockwork gears?" Her face lit up. "Ah, here is the source. There's a saddlebag. The sounds are coming from there." Tabitha lifted the flap of the bag.

Two mechanical doves took flight and began to circle her and the horse.

Jessamine smiled, her eyes following the two birds. "How lovely."

The doves circled Tabitha and the horse together at first, sending off clicks as their circle of flight narrowed to just Tabitha. Then the birds lowered, and a trapdoor sprang open on their backs. A silver thread flew out of one and connected to the door of the other bird as they continued their circled flight, only faster now and lower, entangling Tabitha in the thread before anyone realized what was happening.

"What's it doing?" She cried out as the birds strapped her arms to her side, and the steam horse lowered its head, scooping her onto its back.

Gareth gripped the arms of his chair at the look of panic on Tabitha's face. But before he could react, the horse spun and galloped toward the large picture window, crashing through it and down the lawn. Gareth leapt from his wheelchair.

Grandfather rushed in. "What in the blazes?"

"Tabitha," Jessamine answered, her face pale with shock.

Together they raced to the window. Gareth's thoughts of hiding his ability from Lord Pensees were lost in the moment. He followed the horse's path out the window as Jessamine pulled the flap in her corset, releasing her wings. She leapt and grabbed hold of him as he climbed higher.

"Tabitha?" Grandfather shouted his question after them.

Steam rose in a white puff behind the silver horse as it galloped full speed for the woods. A dark cloud hung low over the forest, giving birth to a foggy vapor, oozing its way between the trees. The ghastly sight appeared like a scene from a gothic novel. Gareth had pushed the ominous thoughts from his mind and aimed right for the horse when arrows began to rain down around them. Jessamine quickly flipped herself in front of him, hugging his body with her arms and legs as they rolled around to avoid the onslaught of arrows.

"All my clothes are fabric armor," Jessamine shouted breathlessly at him. He ducked them into a patch of bushes to remove them from the path of the arrows.

Once in the bushes and out of their range, they sought out the direction of the steam horse and Tabitha, but neither were anywhere to be seen.

Gareth shot up in the air. "We've got to find her."

Jessamine, unable to follow him up, shouted at him. "Get back down here. You don't have your armor on. We have to go back to the house for help. Sarah and Thompton will know what we need to do."

The crunching of leaves drew Gareth's attention to the footsteps behind them. Lord Pensees stumbled through the open field, sweat beading his forehead. His blue eyes were wide and panicked as he headed toward them.

"Grandfather!"

Gareth zoomed out to stop Lord Pensees from charging into the forest. An arrow whistled through the air, the feathers nearly brushing Gareth's ear. The morning sun glinted off the steel arrowhead the moment before it sunk itself into the old man's chest. Jessamine's scream sounded muted and distant in Gareth's ears. He froze in shock. Blackness closed in on the periphery of his vision as it narrowed on what he saw. He sunk toward the ground, his knees buckling under him.

Jessamine grabbed Gareth and shook him out of his trance. She climbed on his back. "I'll shield us both. You fly us to your grandfather so we can get him to the house."

Gareth shook his head and swallowed. His eyes darted toward the ominous dark fog filling the woods to overflowing. "Tabitha?"

"Lord Pensees is hurt. We need to tend to him and get help. If you go after her alone, you're going to get yourself killed, and then you won't be able to do anything for Tabitha."

He swallowed and reluctantly nodded. Reduced to hiding behind his wife's skirt. *Not anything a man ever wants to do.* He bit down on a curse and flew them out of the woods to his grandfather.

Blood bubbled on the old man's lips. Grandfather's eyes had taken on a far-off look. Gareth scooped the man's limp body into his arms. In a harsh whisper Grandfather asked, "Where's Tabitha?"

Gareth swallowed his heart as it rose in his throat. The man was heavy in his arms, and his wife clung to his back. Sweat beaded on his forehead as he made Waverly Park his focus. He just needed to make it there

Jessamine whispered in his ear, "We'll get help and we will find her. We will. We have to."

Her words echoed his thoughts. He had to rescue Tabitha, if it was the last thing he did. She had no part in this war, and he would make damned sure she wasn't a casualty of it.

Chapter Sixteen

Gareth and Jessamine entered the house by way of the kitchen, placing Grandfather on the table.

"Sarah!" he shouted as they entered. "Sarah!" He flew around to the pantry looking for her.

She came running in from the hall. "What is it?"

"Lord Pensees has been shot, and Tabitha's been kidnapped."

Sarah grabbed at her chest, her mouth and eyes echoing Gareth's own sense of horror. Her face grew pale. "When? How?"

"I'll tell you all in a moment, but first, Grandfather." He pulled the ruddy woman to the table. "Can you help him?"

Gareth moved back and stared at his grandfather's lifeless body as Sarah bent over to look more closely at the arrow and to listen to his chest. She bent over his face, putting an ear to his lips.

The cuckoo clock above the stove must have been ticking, but Gareth could not hear it for his own heart pounded in his ears. Sarah had been baking. The coppery smell of his grandfather's blood mixed with the sweet scent of bread and revolted him. Tears stung his eyes, and he swallowed back the bile which wanted to rise. He could not allow the full gravity of this moment to reach the surface. He'd never acted like a blubbering fool and now was not the time to start. Something touched his hand. He blinked at Jessamine beside him and felt her hand intertwine with his. He said nothing but didn't stop her either.

Sarah rose up, her eyes wet and her face grim as she shook her head. "I'm sorry."

Gareth clenched his jaw and worked to steady the quiver in his lips. "Tabitha can still be saved, and we must." He swallowed again.

"How was she taken?" Sarah asked as she picked up a table covering and draped it over the body of Lord Pensees.

Turning from the sight, Gareth answered, "The gift was a trap. Some kind of mechanical horse and birds that took hold of her and escaped out the window. We followed as far as the woods before being assaulted by archer attack. There was more than one. At least half a dozen, if we judge by the number of arrows raining down on us."

Sarah marched to the pantry and pulled open a door. She grabbed hold of a shelf of canned vegetables and pushed it forward, revealing a passageway. "In here, quick."

Gareth stayed back. "I'm not hiding while they fly off with Tabitha. We must go after her."

Sarah turned back to face him, her own eyes red and wet. "I know. I've taken care of the girl since the day she was born and placed in my arms as a wee babe. She's like me own. But we canna go running off unprepared. Come. This be a passageway to the stables. Thompton will be there and our weapons."

Gareth and Jessamine followed, ducking as they entered the passageway.

"What about my father? We can't leave him defenseless," Jessamine asked as they followed Sarah into the long dark corridor.

"Mr. Keller went into town early this morning to sign the final papers with the solicitor. He plans to stay with his sister's family tonight and come get Tabitha for the voyage tomorrow."

Gareth grabbed up Jessamine. "Wouldn't we move faster by flying?"

Sarah's feet left the ground. "Aye, I was na thinking. Living among humans, I've grown accustomed to walking."

They raced down the deep stairwell into total darkness.

"Hold on." Sarah threw a handful of something into the air. A glowing powder lit the path ahead of them in a rainbow of glittering light. "Fairy crystal dust. I dona need it. I've memorized the way but dona want the two of ye gettin' hurt."

They came to another set of stairs which led to a trapdoor above. Sarah pushed it open and they came up in the storage room of the stables.

"Thompton!" Sarah screamed as she pushed away rakes and pitchforks before opening a large crate.

Thompton was not in sight. Sarah grabbed a quiver and filled it with arrows before swinging a longbow onto her shoulder. She glanced up at Jessamine. "Do ye know how to wield a sword?"

Jessamine shook her head. "But I can throw knives. I learned from the Cherokee near our home. They used to come play in our yard when we were children."

"Good. Here." She grasped three knives and handed them over to Jessamine, who quickly lifted her skirts and tucked one into each of her garters and the last in the straps of her corset.

Thompton entered the room. "What's the ruckus 'bout?"

"Someone's taken me Tabitha," Sarah answered.

Thompton marched into the room in two quick strides, knocked over another stack of tools from a crate, and lifted the lid. "Do we know where they've taken her?" He pulled out a claymore and strapped it on his back before doing the same with a small sword on his hip.

Sarah turned to Jessamine. "Ye said it was mechanical animals, like the things ye and Tabitha work on in the bonnet room?"

Jessamine nodded. "Yes, obviously by someone of the underground automation movement."

Thompton handed Gareth a small sword to strap onto his side and nodded toward his wife. "I'll go fetch Lord Gareth's chair. We'll take them by carriage to Mrs. Collins's place. If anyone knows who would have made such automatons, she will. I'll drive, and Sarah will sit with me as second guard."

Gareth stood next to Jessamine as the other two finished getting ready.

"So Tabitha doesn't rework bonnets? Do I really not know the truth about anyone?" Gareth scowled at his new bride. The secrets around him had been stacking up like barrels, each concealing their weighty contents. Now, they were jarred loose and falling all over him. Tabitha was his one true friend, and even she hid things from him.

"She was afraid you wouldn't approve. She said you were always discouraging her intellectual pursuits."

Gareth shook his head. "Only for her own good. Too much knowledge and thinking is dangerous for the female mind."

Jessamine crossed her arms and frowned at him. "Superstitious nonsense used to keep women in their place. Only I don't believe pretending stupidity to be a woman's God-ordained place at all. The Proverbs 31 woman is exalted for her business sense as well as her ability to take care of her family and home. Her intelligence brings honor to her husband. Do the English presume to know more than God about a woman's abilities?"

Gareth turned away from her and stared out the doorway of the stable as the two servants exited to make preparations. He swallowed and tried hard to push away the fact that her words made sense. "I refuse to argue with you about this right now. We have more important issues at hand."

Jessamine reached up and touched his face. He clenched his mouth shut, but her delicate fingers pressed against his jaw. Her eyes had grown soft and searched his. "I have no words. I'm so sorry about Lord Pensees. He loved Tabitha. He died trying to rescue her. You can remember him for being brave. We will find Tabitha. She's become so dear to me in such a short time. The only girl friend I've ever had really. Growing up, I climbed trees, threw knives with the native boys, and waded in creeks looking for frogs and crayfish."

Gareth blinked. "My wife grew up in a more manly way than I did."

"You spent your childhood stuck in a chair, locked away from everyone. But you don't have to be that little boy anymore. We will find Tabitha and get all this sorted out with the Faes. And when it's all over, it will be up to you to choose what kind of life you wish to live and what kind of man you want to be."

Gareth gazed into her dark eyes for just a moment, wondering if life really could be different for him if he chose it.

Thompton and Sarah shouted from the stable area. "It's safe to come out now."

Gareth flew to the carriage while Jessamine followed a few steps behind.

Sarah opened the carriage door. "We did a quick fly through the woods. Whoever was there before be gone now. This visit to Mrs. Collins will need to have the likeness of a social call. Na need to involve anyone else in Fae business. Find out who in town might be behind malevolent automation, and we'll search there."

Jessamine nodded as she entered the carriage. Gareth joined her, noticing Thompton loading his chair on the back of the buggy. How he hated that chair. One of the many reasons he hardly paid a call on neighbors. A visit required a manservant to lift him from the chair, into the carriage, and back again. And if the estate had steps leading into the home… It never ended, this feeling of being less than human and not quite a man. He glanced over to Jessamine who watched him as if she knew what he was thinking. He quickly turned away. He didn't like how easily she read him.

***

When they pulled up to the Collins estate, Thompton opened the door and stepped back to allow Jessamine room to exit. Then he pulled down the wheelchair, and just as Gareth prepared himself for the humiliation of being picked up, Thompton said, "Coast is clear if ye wanna get in yerself."

Gareth paused, absorbing the idea. There was freedom in having those around him know the truth. He zipped out of the carriage and into the chair so they could make their way to the front door. Thompton ran ahead to knock and waited for the housekeeper to answer. A petite, blonde woman in black searched the group with wide, blue eyes.

Thompton announced, "Lord and Lady Smyth to see Mrs. Collins."

"Mrs. Collins is in her garden out back. Make your way around, and I'll run ahead to let her know you are here."

Gareth and Jessamine nodded at Thompton, excusing him to stay behind as usual. The two followed the path to the rear of the house where Mrs. Collins rose from her chair, placing her book in her seat. The middle-aged woman gave them a wide smile and left the shade of the tree to greet them.

"Lord Gareth and Lady Jessamine. To what do I owe the pleasure of this call?"

Jessamine glanced down at Gareth as a signal that he would take charge of the conversation. He paused, regarding Mrs. Collins's silver-streaked hair and soft, welcoming expression. Everything in his being felt her trustworthy. He cleared his throat. "We were hoping you could help us with a problem."

The woman's brows furrowed as she took them both in. "Problem?"

Gareth frowned, and his voice became grave. "Yes, it would seem someone sent us a wedding gift with the purpose of harm. As you can see, we are both uninjured, but we are curious as to the source of this gift."

The woman's eyes grew wide, and a hand fluttered to her neckline. "You don't suppose I had anything to do with such a gift?"

Jessamine shook her head and stepped forward to reply. "Oh no, ma'am. The only reason we came to you is because the gift was…" Her eyes darted about as she moved closer to the woman and whispered, "Part of the movement."

Mrs. Collins's face tensed as she peered down at Gareth and then back at Jessamine.

"Oh, Gareth knows and is completely supportive of my interests."

The woman's expression relaxed. "That is wonderful. Having a supportive and understanding spouse is always a blessed thing. Now, tell me about this gift."

Gareth rolled his chair forward. "The gift was a steam horse and mechanical doves. I believe it was engineered to kidnap Jessamine with designs to hold her hostage for ransom. Do you know who might be capable of creating such a thing? Someone in the bonnet club, perhaps?"

Mrs. Collins pursed her lips and raised her chin. "No one in the bonnet club would ever... We are all upstanding women with only one purpose in mind when it comes to our automation—to make life better for all society." Then she paused and looked away and then back at the two of them. "There was a woman who visited a couple of times. She wasn't from our community, and we actually asked her not to return after only two visits."

Gareth blinked. "And why was that?"

"Her ideas for automation were aggressive items of war and not a good fit with the purpose of the bonnet club. I asked my husband to find out what he could about her, and it turned out she and her husband were new money. That in itself is no problem with the bonnet club ladies. We seek to cross class lines. But it was how this woman and her husband had made their money that was the problem."

"And how was that?" Gareth asked.

"In factories that enslave the poor—ones which pay very little and work the people to death. They even employ children, some losing limbs in the production of malicious automations. They will make any product for any reason, no matter the purpose, for the right price."

Gareth adjusted his chair to a different angle. "Can you tell me her name or know where we could find her and her husband?"

"Her name was Mrs. Steel. Her husband owns factories over in Ardenshire, along the river. Sad and ugly part of town. The streets are full of rubbish and dirty, unfortunate children. My husband told me about a meeting he had over in that area with a man who owns warehouses in the district. A very sad direction in advancement when it's used to exploit the poor, wouldn't you agree?"

Jessamine nodded in agreement. "Very sad indeed, ma'am. The whole purpose of industry is to make life better for the masses."

Gareth took Jessamine's hand to indicate it was time to leave. "I want to thank you, Mrs. Collins. You've been most helpful. I'm sorry if we've disturbed you."

"Thank you both for coming by, Lord Gareth. And take good care in keeping this young lady around. She's got one of the brightest minds I've encountered in the club, next to Tabitha's. You are one blessed man to be surrounded by such intelligent women."

Gareth's heart leapt at the mention of his aunt's name. He nodded before turning his chair to leave.

As they made their way back to the carriage Jessamine whispered. "You were downright friendly. I'm in shock."

Gareth responded flatly, "So am I."

Chapter Seventeen

Gareth and Jessamine mounted the carriage while Thompton strapped the chair to the back. A few miles down the road, when they'd reached a clearing with no cover for anyone to hide and attack, the buggy came to a halt. The door opened, and Thompton and Sarah entered.

Sarah was the first to speak. "So what did ye learn?"

Gareth leaned toward her. "There is a Mr. and Mrs. Steel over in Ardenshire, in the business district. They are known to make malevolent automatons. We need to make haste to Ardenshire."

Sarah nodded in agreement, but Thompton shook his head.

"Sarah, we need to remember what our purpose be." He motioned to Gareth. "We're here only to guard and return King Tristan the second, to the throne of the Court of Ansleigh. I know ye be attached to the human-girl child, too, and so am I, but she isna our responsibility." He motioned toward Jessamine. "I know ye have championed this match, too, but we also know the court will most likely demand an annulment. The fact Lord Gareth be half human is already an impediment to many. Heirs more human than Fae decrease our chances of placing him on the throne and avoiding all out war. Let's na forget our true purpose. Perhaps we have entangled ourselves in the problems of humans far more than we should have."

Sarah turned on her husband, her eyes wide with rage. "Are ye suggesting I abandon Tabitha to whoever has taken her? We know it likely be someone working with the Unseelie, so this be a Fae problem and na just a human one."

Thompton glanced out the window as he had been, staying ever vigilant before speaking. "We dona know the kidnapping is Fae. This happened with automatons, a human creation. This could be unrelated. We need to get King Tristan back to the Fae wood, now!"

Gareth burst into the conversation. "Grandfather's body is waiting back at the house, the selfish old..." Gareth bit his tongue before he spoke ill of the dead. "He never once did a selfless thing in his life, until Tabitha needed to be rescued. I'll not turn my back on her when she's the only family I have left." Gareth scooted in his seat, searching the faces surrounding him for answers.

Thompton shook his head. "If it be a human wanting a ransom, there'll likely be a note at Waverly Park now. We both know the greediness that be in the hearts of humans. Someone has it figured out that the wedding be about new money coming into the Smyth's purse. The wee lass will probably be let go as soon as some human gets his pockets filled."

Jessamine leaned forward, pointing her finger at Thompton. "You defended my place as Gareth's wife to the assassin. Now you want him to abandon me?"

Thompton turned to face her. "I've nothing against ye personally. I was taking King Tristan's side over the enemy's for the purpose of showing me loyalty. But we know from what the assassin said before he died, this marriage'll be used as one of the leverages the false king works to overthrow the Court of Ansleigh."

Jessamine pursed her lips, her face turning red as she spoke. "I'll not abandon Gareth. I've made my vow before God and man on that subject. Does that mean nothing to the Fae? Do you not believe in God?"

Sarah answered, "Aye, we do." She glanced over to her husband. "She be right; she made a vow before God. We are His creations, too, same as man. I'll not interfere with a vow to God."

Jessamine gestured to Gareth. "Nor will he abandon the only family he's ever known to run off with you to a land and a people he's never even seen. You two do what you please and run back off to fairytale land if you like." She gestured to Gareth, "He and I will go after Tabitha."

Gareth took in his wife's ferocity. It was as if she understood his position completely without him saying a word. She was so beautiful when she was angry, but there was more he was seeing, something that drew him to her in a way much stronger than physical attraction. He was so engrossed that he nearly missed the fact Sarah was speaking.

"Thompton, how dare ye suggest I walk out on Tabitha? I'd give me own life before I'd allow harm to come to her. She's as close to bein' me own as I'll ever know. I dona care that she na be Fae. We are loyal to the Court of Ansleigh, aye. But that canna outweigh our loyalties to these who have come to live in me heart."

Sarah patted Gareth's knee. "Thompton'll take word to Tinkton and bring back reinforcements. The three of us will go on to Ardenshire for clues on Tabitha's whereabouts. Then we'll meet the reinforcements at Waverly Park before we continue farther."

Thompton glanced around at each face then back to his wife. He reached out to touch her, but she pulled away.

"Do na be touching me right now if ye value that hand. I'm still angry."

Thompton nodded. He placed his hand under Sarah's chin and tilted her head up. "I know yer sore at me, but I love ye. Be safe. Tabitha be a sweet girl, and I don't want any harm to come to her. I was only trying to look at the bigger picture. If our king dies in the rescue, then what becomes of the Court of Ansleigh? Far worse than the loss of an old man and a girl will come if the false king be allowed to reign. That's all."

He released her chin and started for the exit of the carriage. When he turned about and met eyes with his wife, she nodded. He winked and then grew serious. "It should take me a four-day journey to the Ansleigh court and back. Dona get yourselves into danger until I get back with more guards."

After a curt nod, he took flight. Sarah leaned out the door of the carriage and shouted after him, "Be safe, and I love ye, too. Still mad, but I love ye all the same."

Gareth looked to Jessamine and then back at Sarah who shook herself as she stood outside the carriage. In a swirl of light and air, she became Thompton.

She shrugged and winked at them, and then said in her husband's voice, "Ye don't see many a carriage bein' driven by a woman. We'll be in Ardenshire in about an hour."

Then she climbed into the driver's seat of the carriage, and they started off.

The carriage rocked with the motion of the cobblestone road. A cool breeze blew through the open window. Gareth glanced over at Jessamine. She'd pulled one of her throwing knives out and was eyeing the space in front of her, practicing the movement of a throw toward some imaginary target. Her movements were quick and smooth. He watched, imagining he could see the calculations of how fast her movements should be and where to aim to hit her target. A million thoughts going on at once inside her very pretty head.

He wondered how long it would take to know how she thought, the way she seemed to know him. He'd never considered what went on in a woman's mind before. Not even Tabitha's. Maybe it was this sort of thinking, women as nothing but pretty packages of emotional nothingness, that had put him off on the idea of marriage.

Jessamine turned for just a second and noticed Gareth watching her. She smiled. "It's been a while since I've thrown one. I'm trying to remember what the Cherokee boys used to say to help me with my aim."

Gareth swallowed, not knowing what to say. But then he did. "Thank you...for taking my side against Thompton."

She blinked and drew in a breath as she absorbed what he said. "Of course I took your side. Thompton was in the wrong, and you are my husband. I'm with you in this and all other trials that might come up."

Gareth said nothing, finding it hard to breathe and think in her presence, as usual, so he turned his attention back to looking out the window. She was taking their pronouncement as husband and wife much further than he'd ever planned. If they were to be husband and wife in truth, what would it all entail? He thought of how Thompton and

Sarah argued but remained in love and cared for each other. When Tabitha was found and rescued, he'd have to think more on it all. For now, his young aunt's safety was what he needed to concentrate on.

Chapter Eighteen

They arrived at Ardenshire within the hour. The business district by the river was just as Mrs. Collins had described. Jessamine held her handkerchief over her nose. Gareth peeked outside. Two gaunt boys covered in filth sat in a doorway. Their eyes were as hollow as their stomachs most likely were, judging by their slight, boney frames.

Gareth turned away when he saw a body in the street next to a pile of garbage, flies circling the cadaver, while a man worked to extract the boots from the corpse's feet.

Jessamine's cheeks glistened with tears before she raised her gloved hand to wipe them away. "This is horrible. I've never seen living conditions of this sort." She turned to face Gareth. "How do they stand to go on in a place like this?"

213

Gareth could say nothing. This place was only a few scant miles from his home, and yet he'd been ignorant of it. The look in the eyes of those boys took him back to his own miserable childhood, but never once had he been left dirty, hungry, and in need. It put his personal misery into perspective.

The carriage stopped as Sarah called out in Thompton's voice, "'Allo there. Can ye point me in the direction of Mr. Steel's factory? Me employer's lookin' to talk to 'im 'bout some business."

A female voice answered back with directions to a gray building by the river. Then she said, "Just follow the fog. Ain't nothin' but fog all about the place. Big clouds of it separate off and go driftin,' like that one." Gareth and Jessamine both glanced out the window in the direction she pointed. In the sky was a lone, giant cloud hanging low in the sky. "It looks 'bout as creepy as the tales I hear from the folk that work there."

The carriage moved on. As they drew closer to the factory, fog surrounded the carriage, seeping through the cracks under the door in long, limb-like strands. They seemed to sniff at Gareth and Jessamine before he leaned forward to wave the mist away.

They stopped, and the door flew open. Sarah, as Thompton, stood at the door with the chair. "I think you'll be safe to get in yerself. No one will see ye in all this fog."

Gareth got in the chair while Jessamine made her way out of the buggy.

"The two of ye be careful in there. Have ye worked out a plan?"

Gareth glanced up at Jessamine, realizing they'd not really made one.

She smiled and put her hand to her chin. "I was thinking I'd inquire of them on my father's behalf. We don't know for certain if they were directly involved in the kidnapping. It could be a device they made and sold to someone else."

Gareth nodded. "If that's the case, they'll probably give the buyer's information freely for the right price."

The stench of the river added salt and a fishy odor to the smell of human waste which already filled their nostrils. They started for the entrance to the building. Fog enveloped them and appeared to overflow from the roof of the factory.

Sarah held up a finger. "Hold on."

She placed her hand on the sword still strapped to Gareth's side, and it took on the appearance of a wooden cane.

Gareth glanced up at her. "Can I learn to do that?"

Sarah shook her head. "If ye were a changeling, it would've shown up by now. Na all Fae have extra abilities. This will only look like a cane fer about an hour without a recharge from me."

Sarah, Gareth, and Jessamine made their way to a ground-level door where Sarah, still looking like Thompton, knocked and stood back, waiting for an answer. With a long, low squeal, the door came open. A man with greasy hair and dirty trousers stood before them. "What do ye want?" The man curled his nose at them as if they were the source of the stench in the street.

"My husband and I are looking for Mr. and Mrs. Steel. We came to inquire for some special automations and heard that the Steels were experts in the field."

"Can't help you. Sorry." The man turned to go back in when Jessamine stepped forward and called, "We can pay handsomely. My father needs them to deal with some undesirables back in America. It could expand your business across the Atlantic."

The man turned around and swept back his greasy, dark hair with a grin. "In that case, nice to make your acquaintance. I'm Mr. Steel," he said as he gestured above him. "And this is my factory. Come in, and let us talk business. My office is this way."

Jessamine stepped aside to allow Gareth to enter in his chair first. She nodded to Sarah to stay behind. Thompton's visage stepped back, but cast worried glances at them both. She didn't like it, and Gareth couldn't blame her.

The factory was filled with dirty men, women, and children slouched over tables. In front of them were crates filled with metal components. Each person connected one part with a small tool before passing it off to the next person. The people stared blankly while waiting their turn. Each had hollow eyes and expressions and their clothes hung on them like fabric draped over bones. Gareth could nearly hear the growls of their empty stomachs.

Mr. Steel smirked at him. "Glorious, isn't it? They do this all day, every day, from sunup to sundown, with hardly a break. I've found they work better when afraid, so I walk out screaming and yelling every other day and throw one of them out, refusing to pay him or her for the work they've done for the week." The man inhaled deeply. His body appeared to strengthen as he did it. "Wonderful smell, the scent of human toil, don't you agree?"

Gareth only glared at the man as they entered his office.

A woman with stringy hair hanging out of a jumbled bun atop her head stood by the window, inhaling deeply, just as Mr. Steel had done.

"Darling, look. We have guests."

The woman jumped back from the window and grinned. "Now, this is a surprise. Please, come in."

Mr. Steel shut the door behind him. "They knocked at the door, looking to buy automations."

Jessamine chimed in. "Yes, you see, my family owns factories in America. They've been acquiring old cotton mills and automating them. But there are some in charge of the local town who are complete luddites, throwing up roadblocks to progress at every turn. My father believes it would be much easier if those in his way just…disappeared. I've heard you produce automatons which can help with such a cause."

Mrs. Steel made her way to a tea service, poured a cup, and placed it on a saucer. "One or two sugars in your tea, Mrs…?"

Jessamine swallowed and glanced down at Gareth. "Blythe. Two please. My husband is from here originally but has joined my family's business in America."

Mrs. Steel presented the tea to Jessamine before turning to Gareth. "And how do you take your tea, Mr. Blythe?"

Gareth waved her off. "I've no taste for tea at the moment."

Jessamine sipped her cup. "Do you have some automatons we can see? Maybe get an idea of what you offer?"

She drew another sip from the tea.

Mr. Steel smiled as he moved forward. "Perhaps we have something on the roof you'd like to take a look at."

Jessamine glanced over at Gareth, concern in her face.

Gareth spun his chair to face the man better. "The roof would not be possible for me. Perhaps you could bring them down here."

Mrs. Steel marched forward to Jessamine, taking the cup from her hand. "Let me take that before you drop it."

"Why would I drop it?" Jessamine suddenly blinked and reached out to clutch Mrs. Steel's arm. Her words slurred. "I'm not feeling quite myself."

Gareth pushed his chair toward her, but Mr. Steel stopped him. The man placed a foot upon one of the wheels. "Stay right where you are, Mr. Blythe, or do you prefer Lord Smyth?"

Gareth grasped at the sword on his hip.

"Maybe we should just let her fall." Mrs. Steel let go of Jessamine and pulled her stringy hair over an ear.

Gareth flew out of his chair, catching Jessamine the moment before she hit the floor. He placed her down safely and spun with sword drawn, glaring at the couple.

Mr. Steel danced a jig and ended with a dramatic flourish. "Yes, bow to the king of the Seelie. The crippled mutt the Ansleigh court wants on the throne."

Gareth stood between Jessamine and the Steels, sword ready.

"What have you given her?" he shouted. His eyes darted between the two.

Mrs. Steel replied with a gloating smile, "I don't answer to you. Too bad you weren't in the mood for some tea, or we could've been done with the both of ye."

Gareth's jaw clenched as he lunged at the woman, for a moment forgetting all the techniques Mr. Strong had taught him. There was no focus or aim or strategy—only anger guided his sword. He sliced through the air where Mrs. Steel had just stood, but his lack of concentration kept him from anticipating his opponent.

Mrs. Steel took to the air, tossing the hot tea at Gareth as she made her way to a box on the other side of the room.

He jumped to the side, knocking the cup away.

Mrs. Steel lifted the lid of her box. Mechanical bees of silver and gold flew out and set upon Gareth. The swarm of metal insects obstructed his view and distracted him from his task. He swatted at them with his sword, avoiding the sharp needles on their behinds. They clanked against his steel, slamming into the wall and floor with a thud as he batted them out of his way.

Gareth made his way to the open window, hoping Sarah was close enough to hear. He shouted over his shoulder, unwilling to take his eyes off the Steels as he fought the mechanical insects. "Sarah? Some help, please?"

With the last of the mechanical vermin incapacitated, Gareth flew to Mrs. Steel. The woman and her husband had run to a door on the opposite side of the room, and thrown it open. Gareth flew straight at her, knocking her into her husband, blocking their attempt to escape.

Sarah crashed through a closed window. Glass debris rained upon them and scattered across the concrete floor like the rack of balls on a billiard table. She landed in a squatting position. With a growl, she glanced up, sword drawn and ready for battle. Shards of glass trapped in her fiery hair reflected light like diamonds in a princess's tiara, but the cuts and blood on her arms and the wild rage in her eyes was pure warrior.

The clamor caused the Steels to turn in her direction. Mr. Steel was closest to the window and engaged her. The Unseelie fairy pulled a cutlass from beneath his jacket and took to flight. He pushed in close enough to strike Sarah, but she blocked his attempt with her rapier.

Mrs. Steel, still unarmed, shouted a battle cry, her muddy eyes round and feral as she rushed at Gareth. Her stringy hair flew behind her, and her fingers took on the form of claws. He neglected her the respect due a woman when he kicked her into the wall. She flew into it with a thud. The plaster cracked, and she groaned on impact.

Gareth charged her, holding his sword to her throat. "What did you give my wife?" The word "wife" had a new taste on his tongue, and he quite liked it.

Mrs. Steel spit in Gareth's face before shouting, "I hope she dies a miserable death from the poison I gave her. I only regret you didn't drink any."

Gareth glanced at Jessamine's limp body upon the floor. She blinked at him as her eyes lost focus and rolled back into her head.

"Tell me how to fix her, or so help me, I will kill you myself." Gareth pressed the sword to her throat until a trickle of blood rolled down her neck.

"Never." She growled and pressed her neck into the sword, just as the assassin had at Mr. Strong's. Her body sunk to the floor.

Sarah's rapier clanged again with Mr. Steel's cutlass. Gareth spun in their direction. The man pressed her into a corner, a vicious snarl twisting his face. She leapt over the man in a midair somersault. Steel faked a move to the right before flying straight at her. His dodge took her by surprise, and her eyes grew wide as Mr. Steel knocked her over a crate. She fell toward the floor, and her head hit the crate before she could catch herself. She lay still on the floor.

With a victorious smile, Mr. Steel pointed his cutlass in Gareth's direction. The man's eyes grew as he saw his wife upon the floor. His face turned almost the same shade of crimson as his wife's blood when the realization hit him.

Anger seethed from the man, and his face contorted into something inhuman. He screamed and took a step forward. "You killed my wife!"

Gareth lifted his sword and prepared for the fight.

But the man stopped. His eyes flashed, and a malicious smile curled his lips. He glanced down at Jessamine, still lying helpless on the floor. "A life for a life and a wife for a wife."

Gareth's heart sunk as he rushed toward the man.

Mr. Steel was faster. He flew to where Jessamine lay, sword overhead, ready to bring the point down on her throat. Gareth flew into Steel, knocking him against the wall. Mr.

Steel's cutlass grazed Gareth's shoulder, and the sharp sting made him drop his own blade.

Gareth hovered and then rolled as he had so many times with Mr. Strong, ending in a squat as he glanced at the bleeding slit in his jacket sleeve. He searched for his sword, but he'd flown in the opposite direction. It sat in the shards of glass at Mr. Steel's feet. Swallowing hard, Gareth made for it, but Mr. Steel's feet moved in the opposite direction. Blinking up, Gareth found Steel heading for Jessamine once more.

Panic blinded his periphery with white. He abandoned his mission to retrieve the sword, choosing to fly out over Jessamine's limp body. He beat the villain there and hovered over Jessamine, pressing his chest against hers. He would block her from Mr. Steel's cutlass.

Jessamine's floral fragrance filled his nostrils as he closed his eyes and braced for the pain of the blade slicing through his back. He swallowed and mentally told her goodbye.

Another crash and a bellow forced his eyes open. He glanced towards the cry to find Sarah and Mr. Steel landing on the floor.

Gareth scrambled for his sword and returned just as Sarah stood over the villain with her sword overhead, coming down to pierce him through the chest. The sound of flesh and bone crunching echoed in his ears as the man's eyes grew round and then lifeless.

Sarah sailed into the air and called out, "Are you hurt, your Majesty?" Sarah circled Gareth to inspect him.

Gareth blinked at her. How had this woman lived with him his whole life, and he'd never known her capable of such violence? He shook his head.

"I'm fine." He waved her off as he made his way to his wife. "They poisoned Jessamine." He knelt beside his wife's listless body. A lump caught in his throat as he took hold of her and tried to wake her. "Are you all right?"

She blinked and waved at him, her dark eyes glazed over. Her voice was hoarse and weak. "Go. Find. Tabitha."

He glanced up at Sarah, realizing he'd forgotten all about his aunt for a moment. "They were trying to exit out that door. See where it leads. Look for any other Fae or any signs of Tabitha."

Sarah obeyed.

"Go find her, Gareth." Jessamine turned her head to the side, her face growing pale.

Gareth picked Jessamine up and cradled her to him. "Sarah will look for Tabitha. I'm staying with you right now."

Jessamine didn't answer. Her body went slack, and sweat beaded on her forehead.

"You're going to be fine. You only sipped a little. It will pass soon." He didn't know if what he said was true or not. He traced his hand down the side of her cheek, brushing the stray ringlets which had fallen from her coiffeur.

"Lord Gareth, come up. All's clear. I've found Tabitha and…something else."

Gareth gathered Jessamine in his arms. She was so light and frail, and her arms hung loosely. He choked back the tears which stung his eyes and headed for the door where Sarah had exited. It opened to a stairwell which led to the roof. Once there, he stopped and stared.

Sarah was untying Tabitha, who stood on what looked like a steel ship suspended in air by cables. Above, a silver oblong balloon ran the length of the vessel.

He flew forward, cradling Jessamine to him. "What the devil is that thing?"

Tabitha rubbed her raw, red wrists. "It's some kind of airship. The man and woman put me on it this morning, once the horse took me to the woods." She turned and pointed to the sides of the ship where crossbows with automatic feeds lined the deck. "It was just the two of them, but with those, they could fight like a whole army."

Sarah took hold of Tabitha and hugged her so hard, it looked to Gareth she might be bruising her before she finally let go.

"Did they hurt ye?" She looked Tabitha up and down.

Tabitha shook her head with a half smile. "No, I'm not hurt. Just sore from being tied up."

Sarah glanced over to Gareth. "What happened to Jessie?"

"Mrs. Steel poisoned her."

Sarah approached with her brows furrowed. She sniffed around Jessamine's face and frowned. "Just sleeping herbs. She'll be fine."

Gareth flew closer to the dirigible. "Mrs. Steel said she might die a horrible death. What if they were enchanted, like the herbs you used on Mr. Strong?"

Sarah smiled. "They haven't the power. Unseelie magic is limited. Good can destroy evil, but evil is no match for good."

Sarah examined the ship more closely before turning to Tabitha. "How did they fly it here without it being seen?"

Tabitha walked onto the deck of the ship and pointed to a set of hoses along its perimeter. "These work to produce a cloud cover surrounding. It looks just like the other clouds that come off the place."

Sarah shook her head. "That fog be the byproduct of human suffering. Unseelies feed off it. They're possibly feeding a whole army with those puffs they send off from here. Growing their strength without having to be out among the humans."

Gareth found a place to lay Jessamine, kissing her forehead as he left her there. He flew back to find Sarah and Tabitha grinning at each other in some exchange he wasn't privy to.

"I'm shutting down this factory." Gareth clenched his jaw and made his way back down the stairs to his chair. Once seated, he flung the door to the factory floor open. A squeal and several cries of surprise came out, and the people cowered by the tables, eyes wide as they stared at him in the doorway. He hadn't thought about what the people had heard as he and the Steels fought. He quickly closed the door behind him so as not to show the bodies of their former employers.

"I...I hope..." Gareth thought some more before speaking. "I hope you weren't frightened by the noise. The Steels were demonstrating some of their goods for us, and it got out of hand."

One raggedy woman missing her front teeth peered up. Her straw-blonde hair hung out under a white hat, and her voice shook. "No worries. We know to keep to ourselves."

Gareth coughed and stammered, "Yes, well that's good. But I wanted to inform you all that I've just made the purchase of this factory from Mr. and Mrs. Steel. You are all to go home immediately."

The people stared blankly at him for a moment before stepping away from the tables, their shoulders sagging more than before. One of the women began to cry. Someone in the crowd mumbled about how they would now starve.

"No, no. You misunderstand. You will be paid for the whole day." He pulled his money from his wallet. "Come here and tell me what Mr. Steel owes you for your work."

The people looked at each other and then to him, frozen in place.

"Hurry up. Get your money. We'll be giving you your wages for the next two weeks here while my wife and I reorganize the factory and the working conditions."

The people stood in line, telling Gareth their wages as he gave them money. Most of them were smiling, and one woman broke out into tears as she thanked him. Eventually, they had all made their way to their coats and headed for the door. When he was done, he joined Sarah and the others on the roof.

Sarah was circling the airship rubbing her chin as she did. "Tabitha thinks she can figure out how to operate this vessel. It might be the perfect way to get you and the queen back to Waverly Park without anyone seeing."

Gareth nodded, scooping up Jessamine again, holding her close to himself. She stirred a bit when he lifted her, and he breathed in her scent, closing his eyes. He flew to the ship and took a seat on a bench, cradling his wife. Her eyelids fluttered for a moment but shut again, and she stilled.

Gareth watched Tabitha as she took hold of the controls, flipping switches, sending cloud puffs all around them.

Sarah came and sat by him, both of them watching Tabitha. "We have to tell her about her...Lord Pensees."

There was a glow of pride across Tabitha's cheeks. Gareth leaned toward Sarah and whispered. "Not yet. We'll tell her when we get there. Let her have her moment right now."

Sarah patted his shoulder and stood and spoke louder, "I agree. I'll dispose of the bodies here and meet you at Waverly Park."

Tabitha shot a glance back and nodded to Sarah. "We will meet you there."

The fairy maid ran a hand through her red curls and twisted the hair into a quick bun, pinning it up smoothly. She smiled at Tabitha and hopped from the ship.

Gareth watched the world disappear under them as they rose higher than he'd ever flown. He looked out, imagining the suffering in the streets all around the industrial district. He wasn't yet sure what his newly procured factory would produce. His grandfather would never approve. An Earl did not enter the business of trade. He would discuss it with Jessamine when she woke. She was brilliant at these kinds of things. And she would wake. Sarah had promised. Gareth choked back the emotion boiling inside his gut. It wasn't like him to have so much trouble hiding his feelings. And he hardly knew her, so why was he so concerned? He wouldn't let himself contemplate that just now.

Jessamine moaned. Her brows furrowed a moment before the muscles in her face relaxed again. Gareth gazed at his wife and tugged her closer. She was lovely. Perhaps there was room for a real wife after all. He was already planning to seek her advice on the factory. He could possibly let her into more of his life, *with limits.* He shook his head. *No, no more limits. All of it.*

Chapter Nineteen

The dappled sunlight from the balcony window gave Jessamine a glow while she slept in their bed. Gareth sat in the chair beside her, watching her sleep. Tabitha stood next to him, her hand on his shoulder. Her eyes were red and puffy, and though she still broke into sobs on occasion after discovering her father's death, she refused to leave Gareth's side.

Gareth leapt from the chair and took to flying in the room, a sort of pacing he always did when he felt trapped, shooting back and forth, from one side to the other. "Where is Sarah today? Maybe I should have had the doctor come," Gareth snapped, at no one in particular.

"When you went to speak to Reverend Piper about the…funeral," Tabitha said and swallowed before continuing, "Sarah was here. She propped Jessamine up and spoon fed her broth. She said the herbs in it would help. She's made just as much a fuss over Jessie as you have."

He looked down at Jessamine and thought of how the Steels could have taken her from him. He glanced over at Tabitha, who had taken his place in the chair by Jessamine. Somehow his loyalty that day had switched. He started with plans to rescue his young aunt, but when Jessamine was poisoned, it was her he worried most about.

Gareth turned his attention to the bed when he heard the sheets and blankets rustle. He flew to the other side of the bed and sat next to her.

Jessamine tried to sit up, but fell back into the pillows, her hands fluttering to her face. "My head is splitting."

"Don't try to sit. Just lie still." Gareth pulled the blanket up around her.

Tabitha leaned in closer to her friend. "Do you remember what happened?"

Jessamine glanced over at her, then blinked in realization and again tried to sit up. "Tabitha, you're here?"

"Lie down before I strap you to the bed." Gareth pushed her back down gently.

232

Jessamine glanced up at him, smirking. "That's fine with me but let's at least wait for Tabitha to leave before you do."

Tabitha's face turned pink as she covered her mouth.

"Oh…" Gareth shot up from the bed and hovered to the side.

Tabitha giggled. "Sarah found me tied up on an airship. It's what they used to take me captive and shot arrows at the two of you when you came after me."

Realization swept over Jessamine as she looked at Tabitha. "Oh, Tabitha, I am so sorry about Lord Gerald."

Tabitha patted Jessamine's hand. Her face softened, and her voice cracked. "Thank you. He gave his life trying to rescue me."

"He loved you."

Tabitha's lip quivered as she bowed her head. "I know."

Jessamine tried to push up again, but Gareth stopped her. "Please lie still until Sarah comes back."

"I'm so stiff. How long have I been out?"

"Two days."

"Two days?" This time Jessamine pushed herself up to a seated position, only to lie down again. "I'm so dizzy."

Gareth fluffed the pillow and pulled up the blanket around her. "Rest and take it slowly."

"When you get up and about, I'll take you to see the airship. It's well built. I'm quite impressed with the thing. I got to pilot it here. Wait until you see it."

"An airship? Here? I've read journals on the theory behind them but had no idea any had been built. Take me to it." She tried once again to get up.

Gareth blocked her from standing. "This is ridiculous. You are not going to see the airship right now. You were poisoned. Give it time to fully leave your system first before going off with Tabitha to play with toys." His tone was gruff, but his movements were tender as he settled her back into bed.

"Tabitha, you best go. I think that my husband and I need some alone time." She turned her head and in a mock whisper said, "I'll sneak out later, and we'll take it for a spin."

Tabitha giggled and left the room, pulling the door shut behind her.

Jessamine lay back against her pillow and sighed. "I'm so glad she's home and safe. I'd hated the thought of her hurt in a trap meant for me. I should have been the one to open the gift."

"A trap meant for you but because of me. And if you'd opened it instead of Tabitha, what then? I'd still have gone after you."

"I know, but I'm new here...and not exactly wanted. Tabitha grew up with you. That's all I meant. Had it all gone wrong, I'd be the easiest to lose."

234

Gareth's mouth fell open, and he was about to say something when the door behind them creaked on its hinges.

"Yer up?" Sarah stood in the doorway, holding a tray.

"She just woke. And she keeps trying to get out of bed."

Sarah smiled. "Ye gave yer husband here quite the scare. For the future, remember not to eat or drink anything offered by possible bad folk." Sarah made her way to the table with a tray of tea and cakes before moving on to the bed. She placed her hand on Jessamine's forehead. "How ye feelin'?"

Jessamine sighed. "My head hurts and my muscles ache from lying still for so long."

"Let's get ye up and see if ye got steady legs as yet." She helped Jessamine out of bed and steadied her. "How ye feel now?"

Jessamine took a couple of steps before her legs buckled. Gareth rushed up and helped seat her in the chair.

"I guess I won't be sneaking off for a joy ride in the airship after all."

"Take it easy. We need to be stayin' put until Thompton makes it back anyway. The townsfolk believe Lord Pensees was killed in an accident by a hunter in the wood. If you be up to it, the funeral's set for the morrow." She turned her attention to Gareth. "When Thompton returns, we'll most likely be on our way to the Court of Ansleigh."

"What about my father?" Jessamine asked, stifling a yawn.

Sarah frowned. "I hate to tell ye we deceived him."

Jessamine looked back and forth between them. "What do you mean?"

Gareth leaned toward her. "When we returned from the Steels, we discovered that your father had had an urgent telegraph from your mother. It seems there has been some sort of disturbance with the natives back home. He wouldn't leave without saying his farewells to you, so Sarah…"

"Aye. I took yer appearance and said goodbye fer ye so he wouldna be worried."

Jessamine blinked. "Oh."

Gareth nodded. "He understood that Tabitha needed to stay for the funeral and would have liked to stay himself, but your mother said the problem could not wait."

Wrinkles of worry formed in Jessamine's forehead. "I wonder what the problem could be."

"We can wire them if you'd like," Gareth offered and set a hand on her shoulder.

Her soft smile met his and made his heart flutter. He'd almost lost her just when he'd found her.

"What are yer plans for the factory?" Sarah asked.

Gareth frowned. "I haven't decided. I wanted to talk to Jessamine about it first."

"What factory?" Jessamine asked as Sarah handed her a cup of tea. Jessamine eyed the cup for a moment.

"Dona worry. I just made it. Go on and drink it."

Jessamine grinned and did as she was told, taking a sip before placing the cup back on the saucer.

"I took over the Steel's factory. I paid the workers and told them they could come weekly to collect wages until we had it up and running again. But I've no clue how to run a manufacturing plant, or what it should produce."

Jessamine took a sip of the tea and followed it with a bite of the cake Sarah had put on a plate beside her. "That's simple. Give it to my mother and father to run. Tabitha was going to be my mother's new understudy, and they can decide who will manage it and what it will produce. Maybe it will give Tabitha a reason to come back sooner."

Gareth brightened at the thought and nodded. "Splendid. We'll wire them about the factory, as well. But until then, how do I get the pay to the workers?"

"I'll take it there 'til Thompton gets back. I can send the wire fer ye, too." Sarah made her way to the curtains and drew them shut. "I've been thinking that this may na be the best place for ye. I didna want to move Jessamine while she be recovering any more than necessary, but now that she's up, I think ye'd be better off movin' to a room with no windows."

Gareth nodded. "That sounds wise. I'll help move a bed in there."

Sarah stood with her hands on her hips. "Yer Lord Pensees here, and King Tristan the second in my land, ye'll na be doing any such thing. I'll manage."

"I've not agreed to be your king yet and either way, I'm helping you." Gareth motioned her toward the door with a sway of his head. "Go and find a room that suits our needs, and I'll be there to help shortly."

With a shake of her head, Sarah walked out and closed the door behind her. Gareth knelt down beside Jessamine's chair. "How are you feeling?"

"Better. I'll have to remember my southern manners do not apply when visiting evil fairy folk. I'll sew in some pockets and keep snacks on me for when I'm out instead. But pulling out my own snack still seems so rude."

He shook his head at her. "How are you taking all that has happened since we've met in stride? You've been attacked and now poisoned. This can't be the life you dreamed of as a girl when you thought of me?"

Jessamine leaned forward. "It doesn't matter what I dreamed of before we married. This is our reality. I've thought you the most extraordinary man from the moment we met. And it's proven true. I should have expected marrying you would come with an extraordinary life."

Gareth flew back to the bed and sat. "See, there you go, making it all sound so much better than it is."

"Than what is?"

"Being married to me. I can hardly stand myself most days."

Jessamine laughed. "That was quite honest of you to say." She smiled and pushed herself up in the chair. "I guess it's just how I was brought up. My parents weren't perfect. My mother…when she is on a project, working out the bugs to it, she forgets the rest of us even exist. That's how my father and I ended up coming to England without her. She was supposed to come, too, to help me pick out a proper suitor. But she'd been working on a new automaton for the factory and would not leave her workshop on the day we were to depart. And yet, my father adores her. And she adores him for accepting her when she gets that way. She's sent so many messages to me, apologizing for missing my wedding. I'd be lying if I said her missing it didn't hurt my feelings. But that's the mom I've got. Brilliant and obsessive. She's planning a huge reception in America for when we get to visit, to make up for missing the wedding."

Gareth considered her words before he rose and looked away. "Well, I was brought up that marriage was a necessity for men to produce legal heirs and nothing more. And a wife was a shackle keeping a man from his entertainment, leaving him to always be picking at the lock for his freedom. I've had no interest in the whole matter. Especially with my secret to keep."

"And now?"

He looked back at her. "Now I'm thinking of the way you stood by me, ready to aid me. If marriage can be like that…I might not be so opposed to it all."

Jessamine motioned toward the door. "I think Sarah and Thompton show that's possible. She misses him, you know."

Gareth only nodded.

For a brief moment they just stared at each other. Gareth's heart ached in his chest. "If you think you can put up with me..." He stood and took her hand, drawing her to her feet. "I'd like to try and learn to be a good husband."

He pulled Jessamine to him and tasted her lips. They were soft and sweet from the tea and cakes.

When the kiss ended, Jessamine blinked up at him. "I think that was an excellent start."

"Nothing more until you are recovered."

"And when should that be?"

Gareth clenched his jaw as his thoughts drew dim.

"What is it?"

"Sarah thought you'd wake right away from the poison, but it took two days. It has made her rethink what they poisoned you with. Perhaps there was something other than herbs in the tea. We don't know yet."

Jessamine swallowed and looked away. She forced a smile and glanced back up at him. "I'm sure it was only herbs, perhaps just a lot of them at once. I'm feeling better by the moment."

But Gareth saw the hint of fear in her eyes.

Chapter Twenty

Gareth stood in the bonnet room, looking down at his black, fitted pants and the tunic Jessamine had just had him don.

"I think you'll have more mobility in these than the armor, but the steel threads knit into the fabric will protect you just the same." Jessamine circled him, pulling at the shirt and spreading it out. "What do you think?"

Gareth shot up toward the ceiling, punching at the air and kicking pretend Unseelie Fae. "I like it. It's kind of form fitting though." He glanced toward Jessamine. "Why isn't yours as form fitting as mine?"

"Because I don't want you distracted while in battle."

"And what's to keep you from getting distracted?" Gareth landed in front of her and pulled her close.

She batted her eyelashes at him. "I can control myself."

"Are you sure?" He bent to kiss her, his mouth capturing hers. Her scent, intoxicating as always.

Jessamine pulled away, swayed just a bit, and shook her head.

He frowned. "Are you all right?"

She took in a deep breath and then let it out. "It was just a dizzy spell."

She shook it off and made her way to the work table. "I've made something for you."

Gareth followed her and placed his arms around her waist. "And do you get as obsessed as your mother? Will you be missing for days at a time, locked in here?"

Jessamine joined him at the table. "Yes and no. Yes, I can obsess a bit, but not quite to my mother's extent. I had to live on the other side of the door from her, so I try not to behave in that manner. Also, I'm not as interested in automation as she is. Tabitha is more the sort to dabble in it than me. My obsession has been two-fold. Finding the boy who saved me." She glanced at Gareth out of the corner of her eyes and grinned. "Done."

He kissed her forehead.

"And flying. I want to fly. So far I can glide, but not fly."

Gareth came up and swept her off her feet. He pushed off toward the ceiling. "I'll fly you anywhere you want to go when all this Unseelie fairy business is done."

She pouted. "But that's just it. I want to fly on my own."

She sighed as Gareth's lips traveled down to her ear again and along her jaw.

"Ahmm, I hope I'm not interrupting," Tabitha announced as she entered.

Gareth sunk back to the floor and placed Jessamine on her feet. She pulled out of his embrace and laughed. "Nope, perfect timing."

"Another place where we disagree," Gareth mumbled under his breath.

Tabitha's blue eyes grew wide with excitement. "Did you show him what we've been working on for him?"

Gareth leaned against the wall and crossed his arms. "Did you two fashion me a bonnet to go with my new suit?"

"Not quite, but sort of." Jessamine made her way to a chest and opened it, pulling out a pair of long, cage-like cylinders. "Tabitha and I both were talking about how you can stand, kick, and what-not, but cannot walk. We think it must be something in your knees. We've made these braces with gears and joints to mimic the actions of knee joints. We thought with these, you might be able to walk."

Gareth pushed away from the wall and examined the braces. "I don't know."

"If they don't work, you've lost nothing. At least try them." Jessamine knelt before him and attached the braces to his legs. She stood back and took him in. "Now try to walk."

Gareth swallowed and took a step, slowly raising his foot and placing it in front of the other. He took another and almost allowed a grin when a spring from one of the braces popped out of the thing and shot across the room. He was about to fall on his face when he caught himself with flight. At that moment, the gears that made the guts of the other brace spilled onto the floor.

"What happened? I don't understand?" Jessamine stepped closer, kneeling to pick up the pieces and examine the braces as Gareth ripped them off and threw them to the floor.

"It's the curse. Ye will na be able to rid yerself of it or gloss over it." Thompton stepped into the room from the open door.

Gareth turned to face the man. "What curse?"

"Yer mother, God rest her soul, paid an Unseelie fairy to make yer father enamored with her, and she asked for a first born son...ye as a part of that, to try and win yer father's love. But there's always a price for that kind of magic. A side effect, so to speak. Yer disability's from that bargain."

Tabitha ran up to Thompton and hugged him like a daughter might greet her father, and he hugged her in return. "You're back!"

"Aye. Just got in. Sarah's packing for our journey now."

Gareth moved closer to Thompton and extended his hand, something he'd never done with the serving man before. "Good to see you've returned safely."

Thompton paused and took in the gesture before bowing instead. "Aye, good to see ye as well, yer grace."

Gareth sighed, crossed his arms, and pursed his lips. "What did you discover?"

"The Court of Ansleigh awaits yer appearance. Yer cousin, Tinkton, sits on the throne in yer stead, temporarily, but he's anxious for yer safe arrival to the wood of the Seelie Fae. He's sent guards to accompany us on our journey."

"I've not decided to take the throne."

"Then ye will need to go, regardless, and appoint a successor. Tinkton says he will take it, but begrudgingly. He has no interest in ruling but will if ye canna be persuaded to take it. Sarah told me of Lady Jessamine's poisoning. Perhaps there will be some information in the book of healers back at the Court of Ansleigh. Sarah wants to check them and see what she can find to aid in Lady Jessamine's recovery."

Gareth turned to face Jessamine. A new interest in the journey sprang to life. "I suppose we should go pack. The sooner this journey is behind us, the better."

"What of me?" asked Tabitha.

"You will finally join the Kellers in America." Gareth grinned and turned to Thompton. "See that she is safely booked on a ship for America before we depart and that Jessamine's parents are wired to expect her."

"Aye, yer grace." Thompton bowed again, causing Gareth to bite down hard on his tongue.

He flew into the hall and stopped. Soon he would be meeting his mother's family. Thompton had said, "God rest her soul," so she must actually be dead. He swallowed. She'd brought the curse on him which had made him lame. What else was there to what his mother had done? There had to be more. If nothing else, the journey would help Gareth know exactly who and what he was. But he would not accept the throne. He would not be king.

His mind was made up on that.

Jessamine came into the hall and put a hand on his arm. Beads of sweat stood on her forehead. She dug her nails into his arm and swayed on her feet. Her sudden pallor worried him. What had the Unseelie done to her?

"Are you all right?" he asked. He quickly changed his expression. He couldn't let her see his worry. He'd been an invalid long enough to know how that look was perceived.

A slight smile pulled up the corners of her mouth, and her eyes softened. "I'll be fine."

Tough. As always.

He shook his head and swept her up into his arms. Her eyes grew in surprise and she squealed. "Put me down! I can walk just fine."

With a smile, he hovered down the hallway with her. "Maybe I just want to sweep my wife off her feet."

She laughed and wrapped her arms around his neck. "In that case…" She finished the sentence with a soft kiss.

Her floral scent surrounded him, its comforting embrace also pricking his heart with worry. It amazed him how much he'd come to need Jessamine in such a short time. In the Ansleigh court there would be information and books on fairy herbs and fairy healing arts. The throne did not call him to the land of Fae, but he'd go to make his family safe, and that included Jessamine above all, now. He would find a cure for her and get the war between the Fae courts out of their lives.

For good.

Continue for the story of Gareth's mother…

in

When they entered the vines which separated the wood of man and the forest of the fae, Lady Ansleigh Smyth sat her two-year-old son on a patch of soft, green moss next to a crystal pool. She fell to the ground beside the boy. A mist swirled about them where the cool air met the warmth of spring.

Her arms ached from carrying the fair-haired child. She looked up to the heavens in true thanks and breathed in the woodsy scents of soil and leaves. Tired—she was so tired, but it was worth it. She was home and she'd never go back to that heartless world again.

The boy giggled. She smiled at him, blowing a tendril of auburn hair from her face as she propped herself on an elbow. The warm spring which seeped from the entrance to the forest of fae kissed her frozen cheeks. She wriggled out of her winter cloak. She spread out on the ground, not caring if she got a stain on her saffron dress. Those worries were behind her now. Good riddance.

She leaned in and pinched one of her son's cherub cheeks as she straightened his nearly useless legs. He bounced up and down, while she helped him remove his coat. Tristan's hazel eyes matched hers and twinkled with laughter. He was beautiful, just like his father. Only, her son wouldn't need a title to be a great man. The fae had no need of titles, they only needed their hearts. All that mattered was, in this place, Tristan would be loved and able to give love. It was why she'd carried him up the mountain on Christmas Eve, to be raised in the land of her people. The Seelie Fairy Court of Ansleigh, where love and peace abounded. He would not grow up in the cold, hard world of men. He would leave the threat of winter behind forever.

The tickle in the back of her throat became unbearable, and she gave in to the short coughing spell. Pain rippled through her chest as her heart raced, thundering in her ears. The toxic environment of the world outside had taught her a hard lesson. Her parents had warned her, but she had refused to listen. Then her body rebelled against her. At first she ignored the pain, and did her best to hide it. But soon her constant torment took root in her face and in her skin. Everyone had noticed her body wearing away too early. She outstripped her husband and grew nearly a decade older as each year passed. The fire of passion that had burned in her husband's eyes faded, replaced by a frigid glare of iron.

She coughed and tasted the metallic coating on her tongue. Blood. Once she got home, her mother could heal her and help her son. Her heart fluttered with hope. The winter outside the fae forest slipped from her skin and faded. She hoped the memories would fade as well.

"Bu-uh-fy! Bu-uh-fy!" Tristan pointed towards the green canopy above them.

Ansleigh followed his gesture and watched with a smile as light with wings of many colors descended. "No my love, those are not butterflies. They are our cousins, the pixies. They guard the gate to your grandfather's court."

Ansleigh stood and held out her hands in a welcoming gesture. "Dear cousins, it is I, Princess Seyraed of the Fairy Court Ansleigh. Please allow me entrance. I've need to see my father and mother and ask permission to come home."

253

Small voices squealed and buzzed around her head as they circled. "Our princess is no more. We know the truth this time. We will not be fooled again."

"I am Princess Seyraed. I've been gone for three years, but I've come back. I want to come home. Please!" Ansleigh's voice cracked. She bent and picked up her son. "My son and I have need of my mother's healing powers. Please allow me entrance."

A deep guttural growl from behind broke her plea. She whipped around to face the sound and gripped her son tighter. A wolf shook the remaining snowflakes from its coat and lifted his snout in the air, snuffling. It narrowed its eyes at Ansleigh and howled. Instead of the lonely cry wolves sang at the moon, the howl had a malicious ring. It made the hair on the back of her neck stand on end.

When it ended, the squeaky little voices chimed, "he says you smell of fae coated in human filth. He knows not what you are."

"I am fae." Ansliegh's body shook. Fear intermingled with anger and frustration as she continued, "I followed an Englishman home from a hunting trip in our wood three years ago. I've lived with his family. Please allow me entrance."

The little voices buzzed about, chanting in unison. "We will open the veil, but the wolves stand guard. If you are not who you say you are; you will be devoured."

Two more wolves joined the first. They all let out a snarl and bared their teeth in a display designed to intimidate.

Ansleigh stood tall, relief prickled her skin. She had little doubt her mother would recognize her. She had nothing to worry about. Gripping her son's face to her chest, her voice held steady as she nodded. "I understand."

The two burgundy cloaks lay crumpled on the moss. Part of her wanted to take care of them the way she'd grown accustomed, to fold them, to avoid her father-in-law's glare of disapproval. But if things went right, she'd never have need of them again. Nor would she ever see Lord Gerald of Waverly Park again. That thought alone brought a slight smile. With a sigh and steeled herself, imagining the coats becoming one with the moss in a short time.

The pixies flew to the veil of vines and pulled it apart, creating an opening for Ansleigh and the wolves to walk through. She stepped in and her eyes locked on the most beautiful sight of her life. Her memory of home had not failed her. The tree before her intertwined in symbiosis with the vines and created her parents' ornate castle. Vines wove around the tree's trunk in a perfect winding staircase and led to the upper limbs. The tree and vines united to create terraces just outside the mouths of beautifully arched hollows. Human built castles only wished to be half as grand

Tristan pointed at the castle, eyes bright with wonder. She smiled at her son, and blinked back tears. "This is your new home. Have you ever seen anything more beautiful?"

An adult male Fae dressed in a green tunic and tan knickers flew down to her. Like all fae, his birthright and magic lifted him where he wanted to go. "Seyraed, is it really you?"

Ansleigh stared at his sandy hair and moss colored eyes, suddenly recognizing him. "Tinkdon?"

He offered a reserved smile and nodded. His shaggy bangs fell into and hid his eyes. "Yes."

Ansleigh grabbed hold of him with her free arm and hugged him tightly. When she pulled back, she smiled at her son. "Tristan, this is our cousin, Tinkdon."

Tinkdon pushed his bangs back and studied the little boy in her arms. Her cousin's brow furrowed. "You have a son?"

His grave tone of voice made Ansleigh swallow hard. Would her half-human son be accepted? "Yes, and we've come home. I need to see Mother and Father. Can you take me to them?"

A dark look came over Tinkdon's face and he winced. "I'll take you to your father. Follow me."

Tinkdon lifted off the ground and flew toward one of the terraces. Ansleigh closed her eyes in shame. Her heart ached. To chase her dream and have her wish, she'd given up her birthright and remained tethered to the ground.

Tinkdon hovered and called down, "What's wrong? Aren't you coming?"

Ansleigh sighed. "I'll be right there."

She shifted her son to the other hip and trudged to the stairway normally used by other creatures living in the fae wood. A stair creaked behind her as she started up, and she turned to find the lead wolf following her. Her heart fell. They still didn't trust her. She had aged, but did she really look so different?

By the time she reached the terrace where Tinkdon stood, her heart beat even louder in her ears. Sweat beaded her forehead. Soon she would see her mother and she would be healed. Ansleigh nodded to herself and set her jaw.

She followed Tinkdon into the arched hollow. Fireflies danced above them and lit the throne room better than gaslight. She stepped forward and allowed her gaze to fall on the centerpiece of the room, the giant throne where sat her father, King Tristan of the Seelie court of Ansleigh.

Ansleigh could no longer control herself. Although every muscle in her body ached and her heart beat so hard she was sure it would pound a hole in her chest, she raced forward and fell to her knees. She would have fallen prostrate were it not for the fact she held her son. "Father, I am so sorry. You warned me and I didn't listen."

The tears flowed, but her father's continued silence compelled her to continue.

"I traded my birthright as heir for a spell to make an Englishman enamored with me. This child, your grandson, was part of that spell. The Unseelie fairy said she could not make another love me, but could create infatuation. So I asked for a first born son, too."

She paused again, wanting to peek up at him, but afraid. Her gaze reached his knees before falling back to the floor. The words continued to spill from her mouth, and she hoped he'd continue to listen. "I was certain that I could win the man's love with a son. But the boy cannot walk, and doctors are unable to explain why. But he cannot walk and it breaks my heart watching him stumble whenever he tries. I need Mother to heal him. I need to be forgiven. I don't need to be restored as heir. I just need a home for me and my son."

The hall fell silent. Finally she was spent. Ansleigh counted her breath as it came in pants. Three tears fell from her face to the ground while she waited. Finally she found the courage to raise her chin and meet her father's eyes.

His stern look bore into her and his voice had a hard edge as he asked, "And your husband, did you win his love?"

Ansleigh's head bowed and a lump formed in her throat. She whispered, "You cannot win something that does not exist."

Two steps her father took toward her and she cringed. Fear overcame her for a moment. Though her father had never struck her, her husband had. Then a large, familiar hand gripped her gently under her chin. The musky smell of her father's skin brought back memories which pricked her heart. He lifted her chin. Her gaze met his glowing, loving face. His silver hair and kind eyes were the perfect harmony of color. He searched her face then whispered, "Not just your son, but you also are sick."

He released her chin and she nodded.

"Humans believe it is the hard iron and steel of their world which makes the Seelie fae sick. But it is not. The hard hearts of the humans themselves poisons us. Our hearts are tender sponges and not just organs. They house our souls." He pounded on his chest with his fist and looked her in the face once more. He wiped a tear from his eye and said, "Yours has starved these three years."

Ansleigh shook her head and gripped her son tighter. "But I have *his* love."

Her father looked on her with pity and shook his head. "That does not count. Children are greater, bigger sponges, requiring much more love than they are capable of giving." He nodded as his eyes became glassy, staring into a past only he could see. "This I know too well."

Shame washed over her. His words rang true. Her father had loved her, but she'd shunned it—chasing a love that didn't exist. In the same way, she loved her son more than he could ever return. Still, she pleaded with her father, her voice uneven. "Am I forgiven? Can we stay?"

Her father offered her a hand and lifted her to her feet. He squeezed her fingers in his and didn't release them. "You were forgiven long ago."

She nearly squealed as she grabbed hold of her father, barely making sure not to crush her son. Her father's big, strong arms wrapped around her and pulled her close. She sobbed embarrassingly against his shoulder, breathing in his scent with each breath.

He held her without a word until she finally settled. She wiped her tears as she pushed back from him and held out her son. "This is your grandson, Tristan."

Her father took the little boy into his arms and smiled. His grey eyes twinkled. "Tristan?"

"Yes." She wiped the moisture from her face with her sleeves and searched the court. "Where is Mother? We desperately need her."

King Tristan's shoulders sagged and his eyes lost their mirth. "Your mother is no more."

Ansleigh clutched her hands to her chest as her heart fell into her stomach. "What do you mean? She's not ancient; fae live for hundreds of years. She's not even one hundred yet."

Her father stood frozen in silence for a moment, his face ashen. She waited for him to speak. The weight of what he was about to say filled the space between them. Baby Tristan yawned and settled in his grandfather's arms, closing his eyes. A faint smile broke on her father's lips before he returned his gaze to her. He swallowed hard.

"Your sold birthright granted the Unseelie entrance into the Seelie court. With it, they confused the pixies, and were allowed in. Without warning, the intruders attacked us. Your mother died because she refused to retreat to the castle, determined to heal the wounded left in the wake of the aggression." He closed his eyes. "They killed her."

"No." Ashleigh's mouthed the word, for her remorse left her breathless.

Her father's eyes held no hope. "She was our last healer. There are no others. You were to be next, but..."

The weight of her guilt crushed Ansleigh and she collapsed, broken, to the floor. "No."

"Only those who made it to the castle were saved. The battle took Tinkdon's father and brother as well. We lost so many."

She curled in a ball and gazed out at nothing, taking in all the death and destruction her sin had wrought on her family. An empty hole replaced her heart, though it still hammered in her ear drums.

Her father cleared his throat and shuffled back a step before he spoke again. "And though you are forgiven, you cannot stay here."

Ansleigh blinked hard and rushed to her feet in shock. "What?"

"*I* forgive you, but because of your bargain with the Unseelie, the others will not. Many here lost loved ones that day. The rest of the Fae do not love you like a father loves his only child."

The trembling began again in the pit of her stomach. What will she do? Where could she go? She stared at the babe asleep in her father's arms. Those arms reached toward her

261

and deposited Tristan back into hers. She stared at her father, and her lip quivered.

"I cannot guarantee your safety here." He glanced down at the boy and his voice faltered. "Nor his. I couldn't bear to take you back only to lose you. I've lost too much already."

What he said sunk into her heart and mind. She'd been forgiven but still lost her home.

He threw his hands in the air and returned to his throne. He refused to look at her again. As he sat, his hand reflexively grabbed hold of the ornate hilt of the long sword to his side, and laid the claymore across his lap. He waved a hand in her direction in a dismissive gesture. "I'll send the pixies and wolves with you as far as the first town. Then you must go back to the land of men for the rest of your days."

Ansleigh gripped her son and pleaded with her eyes; her voice would no longer work. She willed her father to look at her and took a hesitant step toward him. The wolves growled and blocked her, filling the space between them. Still her father refused to face her although he gripped the hilt of his sword until his knuckles grew white. Numbness seized her and she turned for the door. Tinkdon's bare feet stood at the archway, but she couldn't abide the thought of lifting her head.

Her actions had killed his father. What could she possibly say to him? No apology could ever be enough. She trudged through the archway and down the stairs.

Her tired feet ached, but her legs moved her forward as though put under a spell. They paused just long enough in the green moss for her to bundle up her son in their discarded cloaks. Because of her feverishness, she didn't want to don her coat. Instead she used her own covering to wrap an extra layer around her child.

She had no memory of her descent down the mountain in the ankle deep snow. The hazy sky grew purple at dusk due to the factories' pollution of the city to the west.

The pixies and wolves left her to trudge the last half mile alone. Sweat clung to Ansleigh's forehead, and she felt so weak. Just before dark, she returned to the inn at the base of the mountain.

She stood on the stoop in front of the red hardwood door and mustered her strength to knock. She kissed her sleeping son on the forehead and pushed back a blond curl. Her heart raced in her chest and her knees grew weak.

The door opened, and she could barely lift her head to the happy greeting.

"Are you alright, Lady Smyth?" The inn keeper's wife wiped her hands on her apron.

She has kind eyes, Ansleigh thought and pushed the child into the young woman's arms. "Please, watch over him for me."

"Good bye, Tristan," she whispered as her knees gave.

Lady Ansleigh Smyth collapsed on the rough-hewn floor. Her broken heart stopped beating. And like her mother, she, too, was no more.

Connect with the Authors

MELISSA TURNER LEE

Twitter: @MelissaTurnerLee1975

Blog: http://melissaturnerlee.blogspot.com

Facebook: http://facebook.com/MelissaTurnerLee

PAULINE CREEDEN

Twitter: @P_Creeden

Blog: http://paulinecreeden.com

Facebook: http://facebook.com/paulinecreeden

For more info on this series,

Keep up to date by joining our mailing list!

http://altwitpress.com